Senior Housing

Barbara Brunk Sharkey

Novels by Barbara Brunk Sharkey

*The Sidewalk
Counselor Stories*

This is a work of fiction. Although most general locations mentioned herein are real, specific details have been changed as needed.

Cover Photos: Barbara Brunk Sharkey

To my husband and best friend Richard.

To my family, near and far,
here now and gone before.

To those who care for others
with patience and kindness.

Herman Melville, *Moby Dick,* 1851

*How it is I know not, but there is no place like a bed
for confidential disclosures between friends.
Man and wife, they say, there open the very bottom of their souls
to each other; and some old couples often lie and talk over old times
till nearly morning.*

Senior Housing

Preface

"I want the pictures."

Ginny Noonan directed this observation to her daughter Lindsay, whose head was buried in the sizable linen closet as she knelt in the upstairs hallway, reaching far back into the endless depth of dark wooden shelving and retrieving shoebox after neatly-labeled shoebox of photographs.

"I know, Mom." Lindsay surfaced for air and surveyed the mountain of boxes she had removed so far. "I could put these all on a disk for you, and then you could look at them on your computer."

"I don't want to look at them on the computer. I want to hold them in my hand."

"But there are so many…." Lindsay's voice trailed dispiritedly.

"Give me any date," her mother challenged obstinately. "Any occasion. I can find the pictures in under three minutes."

"I know, I know. I'm not saying you're not organized. It's just that there won't be this much space in the new apartment."

"Your 35th birthday, 2001. Christmas, 1995. The summer we went to the family reunion in New Jersey. Amelia's first spaghetti dinner—sauce all over herself and the high chair. It's all here."

Lindsay sighed. Maybe the hall closet hadn't been the best place to start. Her parents weren't hoarders. But they were certainly savers.

"I want the pictures."

"Okay, Mom. Okay. We'll keep the pictures somehow."

Chapter One

Two months earlier, May, 2009

Ginny accelerated as the light turned green, driving west on N.E. 145th, thinking about the material she wanted to buy at the fabric store, where a sale of quilt squares was underway. Her thoughts turned to the upcoming birthday of her youngest grandson, already turning seven. She glanced at the fences along the yards at the sidewalk, and a sudden unease came over her as the stretch of road appeared unrecognizable. Where was she? Had she passed over the freeway or not? These weren't the right houses for this section. She tried to focus her mind both forwards and backwards at the same time. Where had she been, where was she going? Just as a small panic was beginning to rise in her chest, the farthest cross street came into view ahead: Aurora. Of course, she was headed to the fabric store on Aurora. A right turn and it would be ten streets north.

Back home, Ginny dropped her shopping bag on the chair beside her sewing machine in the kitchen alcove, gave a cursory walk through the first floor to see where her husband Frank might be, then pulled her folder from its secret spot hidden beneath all the old phone books in the corner of the kitchen counter.

She scribbled a few lines on a post-it note and added it to the collection inside the unmarked file. Along with her small pile of sticky note memory incidents, the folder held several newspaper articles about memory loss. Her favorite was the one about the Ph.D. research biologist in the middle of menopause who one day looked through her microscope at work and couldn't remember how to use it. That story always brought Ginny comfort. Memory glitches were apparently a customary part of the hormonal interruptions of female life, that was all, and things always returned to normal. The fact that she was nearly twenty-five years past menopause didn't bother her at all.

Days later, Frank Noonan sat at his brown Maplewood desk, his checkbook ledger out and a stack of bills to his left. He glanced into the backyard. Spring was here. The daffodils and tulips had faded, but Ginny had planted borders of iris bulbs that were coming on strong. His cell phone buzzed, interrupting his reverie. The name of the third of four adult children displayed on the screen.

"Lindsay?"

"Mom just called me. She can't find the car. Where is she?"

"She's at the Thriftway. Why did she call you instead of me?"

"I don't know. Which car does she have?"

"The Jeep."

"How can she lose the car?"

"Maybe she parked at one end, you know, around that curve in the shops, and ended up at the other. Do you think I should call her, or just drive up there?"

"I told her I couldn't leave work, and she said not to worry, she'd retrace her steps again. I said push the unlock button, and the lights will flash."

"I'll drive up."

"Dad—"

"I know."

"You have to do something. It's getting worse."

Frank rubbed his forehead. "I've been thinking. It's time for our physicals. We could mention it then."

"You'll have to go in the exam room with her or I bet she won't talk about it," his daughter replied emphatically, her concern and desperation obvious in her tone.

"I know, Lindsay. I'm on it. Don't worry."

"Don't worry?? She can't find a bright red Jeep in a parking lot full of blue and green Hondas and Subarus."

By the time Frank had their second car, a sea-blue Subaru Outback, out of the garage and up to the corner, Ginny was making the turn onto their street. She didn't see him waiting, so he circled the block quickly and slid the car into the garage, coming in the back way while Ginny carried groceries in the front door from the street. He met her in the hallway as if stepping out of the den, offering to take the bags she held.

"How was shopping?"

"Fine," Ginny replied, flashing her youthful grin, not looking anything like a seventy-three-year old. "Good sales today. Hope you don't mind cauliflower this week…I got four heads. It's never this cheap."

"Yum." Frank was not overly fond of cauliflower.

"And I found a new cookie recipe I'm going to try. The samples were delicious."

"I think you still have chocolate in the corner of your mouth." Frank reached out and gently smoothed her skin with his thumb. "There."

They unpacked the groceries side-by-side in their usual rhythm. When Frank returned to his office, Ginny retrieved her memory folder, making a new post-it note for today's lost car mishap. It was infuriating when these things happened. One minute she knew exactly where she was and what she was doing, the next, confusion abounded. And then things cleared again. She couldn't understand it, but the pile of sticky notes was becoming ominously larger.

That night in bed as they rested amicably beside each other, reading in the light of their bedside lamps, Frank put his book down and cleared his throat in a way that immediately caught Ginny's attention. He made that particular throat-clearing sound when he was nervous about something; she had certainly learned that in 51 years of marriage.

"I was thinking," he started, then cleared his throat again. "Seems like we're overdue for our physicals this year."

Ginny's heart skipped a beat. Did he suspect something? Realistically, how could he not, she berated herself. Maybe *he* had a folder about *her* with sticky notes pressed against its yellow cardstock insides, too. Who was she fooling?

"You're right." Ginny kept her voice light and pleasant. "I'll call in the morning." She leaned over and gave him a kiss before turning out her light and rolling away from him. She took several long and deep breaths, trying to replace the mounting feelings of panic with a strategy. She needed a good one, and she needed it fast.

Ginny chose an appointment date that gave her enough time to prepare, but not so far out as to cast suspicion upon herself. She found a few on-line memory games and played them religiously during the day whenever Frank was out of the house. She was getting quite quick with States and Capitals. She made a list of the ten most recent Presidents and taped it inside the bathroom mirror above her side of the double sinks. Each night as she brushed her teeth she worked on the list. In her underwear drawer she had the dates of the most important events in the last ten years, including hurricanes Andrew and Katrina. In the pocket of her coat she carried the winners of February's Super Bowl (Steelers beat the Cardinals) and the previous fall's World Series (Phillies over Tampa Bay Rays.) She read the paper carefully each morning and tried to think of one sentence to sum up the news, and repeated it to herself frequently.

On the car ride home after their appointments, they shared their news. Frank disclosed that he needed to go have a mole checked at the dermatologist. Ginny mentioned that she had asked about a few little memory glitches she'd been having. "Don said they were just normal aging. I could spell backwards, remember words and objects, count backwards from 100 by 7's, and follow directions. He said not to be concerned unless it gets worse. Then he could do a full work-up." She gave her husband a reassuring smile. "So that's a big relief."

"I bet it is," Frank replied, the unhappy butterflies that had been churning in his stomach all morning finally coming to rest. "That's great news."

Frank's happy mood lasted until after dinner, when he excused himself from the table to take care of an errant piece of chicken caught between his molars. Out of dental floss in his own medicine cabinet, he opened the mirror above his wife's sink. Dental floss on the shelf. And a list of Presidents on the inside of the door.

Their daughter Lindsay was not appeased by the doctor visit, suspecting her mother had bamboozled their family practitioner whom they had gone to forever.

"You have to get out of that big house," Lindsay mentioned a few days later to her father.

"We don't *have* to do anything but die and pay taxes," Frank reminded her.

"I'm sorry. You SHOULD get out of there now, when the transition will be easier and you can make new friends."

" 'Should' coming from you sounds a lot like 'have to.' "

"Dad—"

"I know, Linds, I know. Don't rush me. I'm working on it." Frank sighed as he placed his phone on the workbench and went back to his woodworking. He was making a bookcase for their youngest grandchildren, girls who were six and four. As he sanded the boards, he thought about his wife, his best friend, his helpmate. Pharmacist by training, she had worked intermittently while raising four children, all two years apart. She was practical and hard-working, and loved nothing better than to whip up a batch of cookies for the grandkids, or putter around in the garden. Not that there were any crops in the garden at the moment, except for the sprouts from the rotten potatoes Ginny enjoyed hurling into the raised beds from the kitchen doorway.

Frank raised his chin to refuse the tears that felt on the brink of falling. Normal aging, he reassured himself. Don had said normal aging. So, despite Lindsay's anxieties, he wouldn't let himself worry about it. Yet.

Chapter Two

Lindsay sat across from her father in the tiny exam room in the ER while her mother was at x-ray. "You have to do something."

"We should have picked up the train track as soon as the girls left, but we thought they might be back again this week," Frank replied, his tired voice reflecting an exhausting evening.

Trying to carefully step through the elaborate Brio train layout on her way to the television set in the living room, Ginny had caught her foot on the elevated bridge and gone tumbling. It had been a long time since Frank had seen his wife in tears, and it frightened him more than he cared to admit.

"I'm going to start looking at places," Lindsay declared quietly.

"You're grown up, you can do what you want."

"Come on, Dad, don't make this so hard."

Frank ran his hand through his curly white hair. It didn't feel right. He had always thought he would know when it was time to move, and now didn't feel quite right. Perfectly normal days would go by with no glitches at all.

The door opened and a wheeled stretcher came through, Ginny upright and having a laugh with the aide pushing her. "The doctor will be right here," she announced, "and I'm pretty sure nothing is broken."

Sure enough, it was a bad ankle sprain and a torn hamstring, but nothing requiring more than rest, ice, support, and elevation. "He said I'm going to be black and blue, but it should be fine. He has two little boys...he loved the part about catching my foot in that darn bridge. He knows the exact piece I was talking about."

Frank smiled as he helped his wife get her pants back on and ready to go. Lindsay shot him serious glances all the way to the parking lot and stood by her mother while he went to get the car.

"Mom," Lindsay tried hard to make her voice pleasant.

"I know, Lindsay. I need to be more careful. Believe me, no one was more surprised than me that my foot didn't clear the bridge."

"No, I mean—"

"And we absolutely should have had Mara and Francie clean up the pieces. But they were having such fun, and you know how Jill is, when she picks them up, it's out the door they go in a whoosh." Ginny made a point to never criticize her daughter-in-law, but her son and his wife's exit strategies after babysitting visits left something to be desired. "Next time we'll do it that way. But they were playing so nicely together and it's the biggest layout they've ever made."

"It's not the track, Mom, it's time you should think about—"

"Here's your father with the car. If you can get the wheelchair up close to the door, I think I can swing over without using the crutches. Isn't this a bother, to be on crutches! Hopefully not for too long. The doctor thought I'd heal pretty fast…by next week even I should be mobile again."

Lindsay sighed, pulling open the passenger side door and edging her mother's wheelchair into a good position. Frank got out of the car and came around to help.

"Thanks, honey. And thanks for meeting us. It was a little scary in the first moments, I couldn't tell how badly she was hurt."

"The firefighters were sure nice, weren't they? And the medic guys?" Ginny added as she settled herself and found the seatbelt.

Lindsay kissed her mom on the cheek and gave her dad a hug, discouraged by the amount of denial her parents were living in. Well, she would start looking, then narrow the search of continuous care facilities to the two or three best ones. Then she'd be ready.

Frank propped pillows under Ginny's left foot and between her knees, as she lay on her side facing his side of the bed. He tucked the sheet and light blanket around her tenderly and turned off the bedside lamp. When he crawled in beside her, she snuggled under his arm, head resting against the soft t-shirt he wore instead of a pajama top.

"That was a close one," she murmured. "It hurt so much when I was lying on the floor. I'm surprised the shock didn't kill me."

"If you haven't had heart trouble by now after raising four kids, I think you're in the clear." Frank kissed her forehead gently. "Now me...you scared me pretty darn good. I could barely dial the phone."

"Didn't you love the look on the firefighters' faces when they came in? There I am, seventy-three years old and sprawled in the middle of a gigantic Brio train layout, and not a child to be seen anywhere? I think I landed on Thomas. I can feel a pretty good bruise coming on my hip. If it emerges in the shape of a little blue engine, you could take a picture and post it. You know, like when people see Jesus in a piece of bread."

Frank relaxed and relished the familiar feel of his wife in his arms.

Her fingers played with the pocket edge on the soft tee-shirt. "I've been thinking," she settled in more comfortably. "Maybe we should consider downsizing. It's an awfully big house for the two of us."

"You don't think any of the kids will be moving back in?" Frank was surprised she would suggest such a thing, she'd always been adamant about staying in their home.

"I don't think so." Ginny clicked through their children. "Pamela's forty-seven this year, can you believe that? She's established in D.C. She'll never move back to Seattle. Sophia's doing well, despite the divorce. Another few years and both her girls will be out of her house. I can't even imagine the size of the catastrophe that would make Lindsay want to move her crew back in. And Robert and Jill are doing very well. With her new promotion and his job seniority, I think they're settled."

11

"Downsize by how much? I'd still need a place for my tools."

"And I need space to sew. And a closet for my fabric. *And* a decent kitchen so I can cook and bake."

"We have to stay in the neighborhood, don't you think? All our friends are here."

"Would we just buy a smaller house?" Ginny rubbed the tee shirt as if it was the smooth silk edge of a baby's blanket. "Or are you ready for something like Lakeview Gardens?"

"Lakeview Gardens is the best place for continuous care. Nice views of the lake. Grocery store within walking distance."

"Continuous care. That sounds ominous, doesn't it?" Ginny pondered. "And I'm not ready to give up the cars."

"Of course not. But it makes sense to think ahead ten or fifteen years and only make one move."

"What about your office in the den? All the stuff in the closets?"

"And the garage," Frank added.

"And the basement. What about the Christmas decorations?"

"And the boxes of old Christmas cards you have down there?"

"Okay, the Christmas cards can go," Ginny surrendered on that one, a sore spot with her husband who could not understand their potential use. "What about your boxes of paid bills?"

"I've read recently that you only have to keep seven years' worth. Or maybe it's three. I guess some of those can go."

"What about the Halloween dress-up clothes? There's four boxes, most of them I sewed by hand."

"The kids might take them."

They were both quiet for a few moments, trying to imagine a future in a smaller place.

"I think we'd still need at least three bedrooms. Don't we want a place for the grandkids to be able to spend the night occasionally?"

Frank reached up and turned off his light. "Yes. We do. Alternatively, we could just stay here. And put the train track away when the girls leave."

"That *would* be a lot easier." Ginny patted his chest.

"Love you." He planted another kiss on her head and disengaged his arm.

"Love you." She reached down and pulled the pillow between her knees into a more comfortable spot. She heard Frank drift almost immediately into sleep, but she lay awake thinking for some time.

Chapter Three

Tess had been Lindsay's best friend since elementary school. Both had married high school boyfriends and stayed in the area. Tess's parents had been loving but each difficult in their own way. Her father had lived somewhere on the fine line between heavy social drinking and high functioning alcoholic, before passing away ten years ago. Tess's mother Betty was a chain smoker, although she had tried to carefully shield her children from the evil habit by never smoking in the house. Hence she had spent many hours outside each day, casually pretending to garden, pulling a weed here and a weed there, occasionally planting bulbs or a new hydrangea, and directing the weekly yardmen to their duties. Thus while the yard was fairly presentable, the household ran closer to chaos. Tess had done her best to help raise her younger brothers, and as an adult spent most of her life avoiding all toxins in food and the environment, trying to protect her body from any more damage than what she imagined was already done by the second-hand smoke wafting in her open bedroom window from the porch below on warm summer nights, accompanied by the clink of her father's ice in a glass as her parents murmured words that started out comprehensible but merged into unintelligible speech as she drifted off to sleep.

Now both forty-three, with their youngest, late-born-after-careers-started children finally in elementary school, Tess and Lindsay were as close as sisters and talked daily, increasingly less about their offspring and more about their parents.

"So there she comes," Lindsay related her mother's visit to the ER, "joking with the nurses as if there's nothing unusual going on. I

14

tried to talk to her about moving as she was getting in the car, but she blew me off."

"Remember how long it took me to get my mom out of her house and into an apartment? Five years after Dad died. And once she got there, she loved it. But, God, it's a process. At least you've started bringing it up." Tess adjusted her hands-free device as she sat in stalled traffic. "The fall must have rattled her a bit. Maybe she'll come around as she's healing. Nothing like a couple days being laid up with crutches to start you thinking about a home without stairs."

"I told her to sleep in the den; that couch converts into a pretty comfortable day bed. But she insisted on going up the stairs backwards on her butt so she could sleep with Dad. She's so stubborn. And she's invented a new RICE acronym that she's embracing wholeheartedly."

"Rice?"

"You know, Rest, Ice, Compress, and Elevate for sprains."

"I'd forgotten. So what's your mom's?"

"Read, Imbibe, Chat and Eat."

"I love that woman. At least she isn't perpetually enveloped in a cloud of smoke."

"I thought your mom said she was cutting back?"

"Oh, she has. I think she's down to a pack a day now."

Lindsay had been approaching her front door with a bag of groceries in hand when Tess called. Now she sat swaying on the porch swing, enjoying the five minutes of peace before she entered the Twilight Zone of parental duties. She could already hear squabbling inside. Having her oldest babysit the youngest after school worked out most days, but occasionally when she crossed the threshold there was evidence a mighty war had taken place. There was a sharp bang and a yell from inside the house.

"I gotta go," Lindsay said. "There could be blood or bruises happening in there."

"Okay, talk to you tomorrow. Don't give up about the move. They'll come around."

Chapter Four

Ginny happily observed her dining room, purple and gold streamers twisted in a colorful arc from the chandelier to the room's corners, her bright birthday tablecloth spread beneath the good china plates, and a three-tier birthday cake on the credenza against the wall.

It was Paul's 75th birthday, Lindsay's father-in-law. He and his wife Joan, his son Mo, (Lindsay's husband) and the three grandchildren were coming for dinner and cake to celebrate. Paul and Joan and Ginny and Frank had known each other for over thirty years. The kids had been in school together since junior high, and Ginny and Joan had worked on PTA events together while Paul and Frank had met constructing wood booths for the yearly fundraising carnival. The kids had started dating in eleventh grade, gone to separate colleges, but stayed together and married after graduation. The parents had been thrilled; not everyone gets to have their friends become in-laws.

A waft of something burning caught Ginny's attention.

"Frank! What's burning?" She hurried to the kitchen, finding her husband bent into the oven with smoke swirling and the blueberry pie he had requested sitting on top of a stove burner, dripping juice over its edges. "For heaven's sake!" She opened the window and headed for the back door, but not before the shriek of the smoke detector filled the house. "They're going to be here any minute—"

"What's going on?" Lindsay arrived in the doorway, followed by her husband Morris and the three kids who all bumped into each other as their mother stopped suddenly after one step into the kitchen.

"It's not my fault," Ginny called defensively, trying to wave the smoke into the backyard. "Your father wanted a blueberry pie even

17

though we're having cake. Help me clear the smoke before Paul and Joan get here."

"Too late!" came a booming voice from the hall.

"What can we do to help?" Joan pushed her way through the crowded doorway.

"Grab something and fan that smoke detector, would you please? Before we all go deaf," Frank yelled as he continued trying to separate the smoking, charred berry juice from the hot bottom of the oven without harming himself.

"Got it," said Paul, a tall man, who with several swipes of a newspaper beneath the detector stopped the piercing warning.

"Thank you." Ginny stopped fanning smoke out the kitchen door. "Well, Happy Birthday, Paul. We're off to a great start!"

"Let me do that." Joan took over the scraping from Frank. "You men go start the cocktails."

With the rest of the family dispersed, Ginny glanced at Joan and they both broke into laughter as the last gob of stinking goo was victoriously separated from the oven.

Lindsay observed the easy repartee between her parents and in-laws. She had always known how lucky she was to be blessed with Mo's wonderful parents, and the fact that they got along so well with her own folks was icing on the cake. She sent her kids out the back door to find something to do and joined the men at the credenza as Frank broke out the glasses.

"What was that all about?" she asked her dad quietly.

"The pie ran over, that's all. Bad timing."

"Doesn't mom usually put a cookie sheet under it?"

"I don't know. It's fine, no harm done. Added a little excitement to the evening, that's all."

Lindsay was about to say something, but her husband shot her a glance and she thought better of it. Equally devoted to his in-laws as his parents, Morris, Mo for short, was aware of his wife's push to get them downsized out of this large house and settled somewhere more reasonable. But perhaps because his own parents had already been through the process with no help at all from him or his younger brother, he assumed Ginny and Frank's change would come in its own good time, without difficult conversations and interference from their adult children.

Lindsay, however, knew the two sets of parents were cut from different cloth. Mo's parents had always loved to travel, had only two children instead of four, and, most importantly, were not particularly sentimental about stuff. They had cleaned out gradually after both boys were launched, and in their mid-fifties moved into a small apartment, gradually increasing their travels as they decreased their work schedules. While it was true they weren't able to keep Mo and Lindsay's children at their home for long periods of time due to the space limitations, they made up for it by babysitting gladly at Lindsay's house instead.

Shouts from the backyard caught Lindsay's attention. The kids had discovered the water guns and were having a full battle. Lindsay did love that on these visits to their grandparents, her two girls, at 14 and 12, discarded their teenage superiority and played with their younger brother, Alex, who had just turned seven. She hoped it would last a little while longer.

As Ginny and Joan cleared the house of smoke, Frank and Paul put the chicken on the grill, and Lindsay unwrapped the quinoa salad she had brought and dug the other salads her mother had prepared out of the refrigerator.

The children traipsed through on their way to wash up. Alex yelled, "Great cake, Grandma!" as he swiped a finger-full of icing from the bottom edge of the three-tier chocolate wonder. Alex had learned early on that a trip to *this* grandmother's house guaranteed a gooey delight at some point in the visit.

"Grandma, where were you?"

Ginny woke with a start, Alex's plaintive voice in her head. Realizing she was in bed, Frank breathing peacefully beside her, she tried to relax against the pillows, but her body was still tensed and on alert from her dream.

Today she had taken the seven-year-old, ever-growing Alex to Nordstrom's for new shoes. Afterward, they'd paused as she bought cute summer t-shirts for all the grandkids. Alex's attention was caught by a display of Harry Potter clothing around the corner, and Ginny had noticed the new dresses in the next department and had wandered that direction. She even had Alex's new shoes in a bag hanging on her arm, for heaven's sake, yet off she'd wandered, completely forgetting she had Alex with her. By the time she remembered she was nearly to the mall entrance, and had to quickly retrace her steps. She found him standing perplexedly with the shoe salesperson.

How she had berated herself the whole way home! She tried to make light of it with Alex, and even stopped to buy him an ice cream sundae, hoping he might forget the incident and not mention it to his mother. That's all she needed, Ginny thought glumly, was more ammunition for Lindsay's worries.

The shaken grandmother had been so upset she couldn't even write a sticky note about it for her memory file, the image of Alex's puzzled face lingering with her all day.

Ginny finished the night with restless sleep, and pulled Frank back into bed when he started to get up in the morning.

"I've been thinking. Maybe we should start to clean out the house a bit."

"Whoa! What brought this on?" Frank slid his arm beneath his wife's head.

"At Paul's birthday party. I realized how happy he and Joan are, how carefree with only the apartment. Not held down by so much stuff."

"I suppose there's no reason we couldn't start getting rid of the things we never use. It would make it easier when we do decide to make a change."

"I could start in the basement, and you could start in the garage," Ginny offered.

There was silence as they envisioned the mounds of stuff in each area.

Ginny felt overwhelmed even thinking about it. "Maybe we need a rule, a guideline or something."

"Okay. Like what?"

"Like only keep the best. Or keep the ten best, something like that."

"Does that mean the ten best tools, or the ten best screwdrivers?"

"Do you have more than ten screwdrivers?"

"Oh, yes." Frank envisioned the peg board wall above his tool bench.

"Well, I think it means keep only the best ones that you use the most."

"But that's the point of having so many tools, for that occasion when you need a certain size, you've got the right one at hand."

"You're not making this easy." Ginny looked up at his face.

"What about all your flower pots? Are you only going to keep ten?"

"Well, I might have been thinking ten of each size."

"You see the problem."

"I do," she sighed.

They lay quietly together.

Frank tried again. "I saw in the AARP magazine, that one way to clean out is to take pictures of the things you're attached to, then you can put it all in one album and look at it whenever you want to. So say with the Halloween costumes, you'd have them all right there at your fingertips."

"So you're going to get a lot of satisfaction looking at a picture of your new hand drill rather than holding it in your hand?"

Now Frank sighed. "It's impossible, isn't it?"

Ginny wanted to agree, to take the easy way out and once again say, oh, let's not worry about it. But the vision of her grandson standing forlornly in the shoe department stayed with her, and she knew they had to do something.

"Let's try. The three pile thing. Save, give away, and trash."

"Or yard sale. We could have quite a yard sale."

"Let the kids come through the week before and take what they want, then sell the rest?"

"Sure. It's better for things to be used than to sit around here."

"Okay. That might work." Ginny threw off the covers and hopped out of bed. "Today we begin!"

Frank laughed and looked at the clock. "It's 7:13. I give your enthusiasm till 9:00 to diminish."

"You're on."

After eating breakfast, reading the paper, and dressing, Ginny started in the basement at 8:00 and was exhausted and overwhelmed by 8:30.

She wandered out to the garage and stood in the open doorway, surveying the piles of stuff. One side of the garage was rather neatly organized around Frank's tools and woodshop, with room for one car. The other side was crammed with boxes and…stuff.

"So how are you doing? Any piles yet?" she inquired.

Frank had a screwdriver in hand and was tightening up something on his pegboard tool holder.

"I thought I'd start by clearing off my workbench. If I can get everything back in its place, then I'll know what I really have."

"How did we get all this stuff anyway?"

"We've been married over 50 years and lived in this house for forty-three. I think it comes with the territory."

Ginny edged over to the cluttered side of the garage and pulled open a box. Most everything was marked: Sand Toys. Mason Jars. Rope.

She moved a few more boxes until she hit an unmarked heavy one that wouldn't budge. She opened the flaps.

"Look, here's a whole case of motor oil. Why would that be here?"

"I probably got it on sale one year."

"But why haven't we used it?"

"Oh, at some point they changed from the old weights to the new silicone ones, I was probably afraid to use it in the new car."

"That's now an old car."

"Right. Well, that's one box that can go in the sell pile. Someone might be able to use it." Frank hauled the box into an empty space in the middle of his cleaner side. "I guess we can park in the driveway for a while." He observed his wife digging further into the stack. "Not that I don't appreciate your help," he interrupted her, "but how's the basement coming?"

"I gave up. Too hard."

"It's only 8:35!"

"I know, you win." Ginny looked at him sadly.

"Come here." He gathered her in his arms. "I love you, you know that, right? Don't worry, we'll get it done. Bit by bit. There's no rush."

Ginny rested her head against his chest, tears welling. She wasn't sure, but in fact she did feel some urgency. Some horrible shadow felt like it was stalking her at times, and she didn't know how to get away from it.

"Why don't we quit for today and go get some coffee at Starbucks? And something especially bad for our health that we'll regret tomorrow?"

"If we walk over there, it will balance the sugar a little. We won't have to regret it as much."

"Deal."

It had been a tough start, but the next morning went a little better, Ginny held out till 9:30 and had created her three piles. The "Give Away" pile had only one bag of old clothing in it, while the "Keep" pile took up a quarter of the basement, and the "Throw" pile filled one small trash bag. But it was a start.

By the end of the week, she was so sick of stuff that suddenly the balance was reversed. The "Give Away" stack grew larger and larger, she was generous with what she thought could go straight to the trash, and the "Keep" pile kept shrinking as she pulled something from it each time she walked past. Frank was having equal success in the garage.

As they lay in bed that night, Ginny broached the subject that had been on her mind all week.

"What do you think now? Should we stay here? Or should we pitch it all and move? Make a clean start at a continuous care place like Lakeview Gardens? Prepare for the next two decades? They have independent apartments over there. The ads look nice."

"*Now* what brought this on?" Frank moved his arm so she could snuggle against him. "I thought we were just cleaning out here a little."

"I don't know. It still feels so overwhelming, part of me wants to start fresh in a new place."

"You realize you're still in the basement and I've only done half the garage. We've got a two story, four bedroom-plus-a-den house to work our way through. Technically, we've only sorted the stuff we pretty much haven't used for the last ten years. We haven't even gotten to the things we actually use and want."

"I know. You make a very good point."

"Why don't we just keep going. See where we are in another week."

But in another week, Ginny's progress had slowed. She had had two memory incidents. In one, she ended up at the bank with no idea why she had gone there; in the other, she went to the store, list in hand, but no purse. Luckily she missed the weight on her shoulder as she walked into the market, and drove home to retrieve it before having an embarrassing scene at check-out. But there was no denying it, these incidents took a toll on her feeling of well-being. A reasonable person would have simply returned to the doctor with the new concerns, but not Ginny. Certain more medical scrutiny would only make things worse, she was jumping ahead to preventive care. With less to think about in a smaller home setting, perhaps her brain would work a little better.

But the house. It was overwhelming, even with the three pile system.

After several more futile days with less sorting and more walking to Starbucks, Ginny knew there was only one thing left to do: Call Lindsay.

Lindsay, who had conscientiously begun investigating five continuous care facilities within 20 miles of her parents' home, was astounded to get her father's call requesting her assistance to help them downsize in preparation for a possible move. She was happily shocked that her parents, on their own, had chosen one of her top three facilities, although sight unseen. So a preliminary visit to Lakeview Gardens was first on her list before she attacked even a single closet in their house. She spoke to the marketing director, Iris Harrison, and made an appointment to bring her parents over for a tour.

Pulling into the visitor's parking space in front of the large brick building, an unexpected pang grabbed Lindsay's chest at the sight of a few elderly residents with walkers and wheelchairs making their way along the sidewalk. For months she had been pushing for a move, but now that it was in front of her, uncertainty mounted. She heard her mother sigh in the back seat.

Long used to the emotional roller coaster of these two women whom he loved, Frank sensed the estrogen levels rising precariously in the car. "I think the independent apartments are around the back," he said cheerfully. "This is the main entrance, I believe, but off the lobby it leads right into assisted care. Makes an easier exit out onto the grounds for those with mobility issues. The gardens are gorgeous, don't you think, Ginny?"

"Hmm. Yes, they are. Maybe they have a garden club."

"The residents do most of the flower beds," Frank continued. "There's even a big vegetable garden in the back. And waist-high raised beds on the patio for easy access."

"From where are you getting all your information, Mr. Tour Guide?" Ginny asked testily.

"The website. Quite interesting."

Lindsay hopped from the car and held the door for her mother. The entrance approach was a smooth, gentle rise with handrails leading to automatic doors, a green awning protecting the path. Inside the door, a welcoming lobby stood across from the check-in desk. Administrative offices appeared to be in one direction; signs pointed to the assisted living section down another; and the third hallway was filled with light as if ending in an atrium of some sort.

Lindsay spoke with the receptionist while Ginny wandered over to the bulletin board, which was cheerily decked out in Fourth of July colors and bursting with notices of upcoming activities: picnics, concerts, the fireworks, book groups, knitting circles, lecture series, church services, exercise, movie nights, game nights, cooking, current events, arts and crafts, ice cream socials. It went on and on.

Ginny's eyes dropped to an end table beside the overstuffed couch upholstered in soft blues and greens. Beside a full-flowering, bright red gloxinia, a small round vase contained a turquoise Beta fish. The poor thing floated belly up, dead as a doornail. "I thought they did away with these little container pets," Ginny murmured crankily. "Decorative fish, indeed." But she wouldn't mention it to the others right now. She didn't want to appear to be complaining first thing through the door.

A petite, dark-haired woman approached, and Lindsay introduced Iris Harrison, who warmly greeted them and led the way to her office. After a half-hour general chat about the facility and finances, they took the tour from the uppermost floor dining room, with its view of Lake Washington, through the gym, health center, library, computer room, game room, and activity center. Built at the top of a hillside, the independent apartments along the back of the building had views of either the nearby green belt or partial views of the lake.

Iris pulled a key from the lanyard around her neck and led them into a third floor apartment, explaining the tenant volunteered on the hospitality committee and was happy to have her apartment be shown. A large and spacious living room, a dining room area that looked like it would fit their table; an adequate kitchen with lots of storage space and fairly new appliances; two large bedrooms that would easily fit a queen bed or twins, plus room for dressers and even perhaps a sitting chair. A large bathroom, its elegance only slightly diminished by handrails in the tub and a high seat on the toilet.

"Now the three bedroom," Iris was explaining to Frank, "has another room here," she indicated a space off the short hallway. "It's not quite as large as these bedrooms, but works as a guest room or den."

"And parking?" Frank asked.

"One stall under the building with a small storage unit attached. And one space around the parking circle out back. If you don't need

27

both, then you only need pay for one. Many people bring both cars, then give one up once they see how convenient everything is."

After the apartment walk-through, they ended up back on what Iris referred to as Main Street. With a ceiling of all glass and one atrium wall, it was an area filled with light and boasting a small café with a lunch menu and soda fountain, a hair salon, a bank ATM, a post office, and finally, a small store, selling gifts and food basics like bread and milk. The chapel with three various denominations' church services posted was down the hall. Frank was impressed; he could see how easy it could be to live here and never leave the building. In twenty more years, it might be perfect for him.

As if reading his thoughts, Iris lowered her voice. "You two will be among the younger and most active residents here. But you know, one slip and fall and you'll be glad you're out of your big house with stairs. I can't tell you how often it happens that way." She smiled encouragingly.

"I'd rather take my chances on the Brio set," Ginny said to no one in particular.

"What was that, Mom?" Lindsay turned to look at her mother, wondering how she was taking all this.

"Nothing, dear. It's lovely. All of it. Simply lovely."

That night in bed, Frank cradled Ginny and let his thoughts roam back to the tour.

"So what did you think?" Ginny asked. "The honest truth."

"Well," Frank took his time, trying to think of the positives. "I think people are very happy there."

"People older than us."

"Not all of them."

"I didn't see a lot of people like us standing on two feet."

"They were probably off and doing things out of the building. Or else there are a lot more slip and falls in the world than I realized."

"They probably wax the floors extra."

Frank began to protest, but she cut him off. "I'm sorry. I didn't think it would be like this."

"The question is, do we go when we're making the decision on our own, or do we wait until someone else is making the decision for us?"

"Why can't we just stay here and die in the basement?"

"Suppose we do become less mobile. We could remodel the first floor…make the sewing alcove and den into a big master, make the powder room into a full bath. We could live on one floor, don't you think?"

"And all that empty house upstairs?"

"Live-in help."

Ginny thought about it. "But the kids. You know they'd just worry about it. Lindsay would be over here every day and Robert would fuss about finding the right care. And full time help would be exorbitant."

Frank kissed her forehead. "Then how about we just stay healthy?"

Ginny sighed. "That's not terribly realistic. No, we have to move ahead. Lakeview Gardens was lovely. It's a new chapter, that's all. We'll make friends there. We won't be stuck, we'll do our same routine. We'll still go to our church. I'll help with the shelter meals. You'll volunteer. I'll play Duplicate Bridge once a month. We'll go out with friends. And make new ones. If we can swing that three bedroom, the grandkids can still come to spend the night. It's just a different place to sleep, that's all."

"Okay then. Forward march."

"Forward march," Ginny repeated their favorite catch-phrase, used many times over the years when seemingly insurmountable challenges lay ahead of them: four kids under six, ill parents, an unexpected loss of income right when she became pregnant with Lindsay. And they always made it through. *Forward march.*

Chapter Five

Mo observed his wife Lindsay's "unhappy" face across the breakfast table. "What could possibly be wrong at only seven-thirty in the morning?" he asked amidst the unusual calm of their three children all apparently taking care of themselves elsewhere in the house on the sun-filled summer morning.

"It's Mom and Dad. Something's up."

"I thought you said the walk-through went well. I thought they liked Lakeview Gardens. You should be ecstatic. This is what you've been hoping for, they want your help to downsize and move."

"I know, but it's too easy. I'm missing something."

Mo studied his wife's worried frown with practiced patience. "You've won, honey. Be a gracious winner and hop to and help them without worrying about it."

Lindsay sighed. "You're right, I know. Something feels off, I can't put my finger on it. They must have been thinking about it for some time. They've almost got the garage and basement done, and Dad had winnowed their choices to the Gardens. You know my parents. Wouldn't you think they'd have been more particular, put up more of a fuss?"

"Maybe they worked it out between themselves. It sounds like my dad's birthday party gave them a nudge…you know, seeing how happy my folks are in the apartment. Sometimes you have a wake-up call."

"I guess." Lindsay wasn't totally convinced, but fussing about it would do no good. The better plan was to enlist her siblings and get the house cleaned out before her parents changed their minds. Yes, that would be the new goal. Once their stuff was gone, there'd be no turning back.

Chapter Six

After the impasse with the photographs, Lindsay decided perhaps they should start with the biggest details rather than the smallest. Using the facility's layout for a three bedroom apartment, Lindsay and her parents carefully measured their favorite pieces of furniture and then sat down and decided which would go with them and which could be offered to the families and older grandchildren for future apartments. Lindsay marked all the furniture to be kept with a piece of blue painter's masking tape. That left a rather frightening amount that needed to be dealt with.

They started in the least full guest bedroom, and made their way through the other rooms. Lindsay was amazed at how much she and each of her siblings had left behind in the backs of the closets and dresser drawers: doll collections, musical instruments, elementary school projects, craft materials, college notebooks, and sports trophies.

As all the photographs would be moving to Lakeview Gardens, the rest of the hallway linen closet was less difficult. They would only need sheets for the master bedroom and the guest room twins, and no more than six sets of towels. They ran into some trouble with the tablecloths. Ginny had always collected favorite fabric designs in two-yard lengths, hemmed them and used them on the table. Surely they wouldn't need thirty tablecloths in the new place, Lindsay encouraged her mother. She finally convinced Ginny to pick out her ten most favorite patterns, with an extra five holiday fabrics thrown in, and to put the rest in the "Give Away" pile. Lindsay stuck two of her own personal favorites in her take-home stack by the front door.

The children's game and toy closet was difficult, as Ginny was not ready to part with beloved and carefully saved Fisher-Price and Playmobile sets, insisting the airport and farm pieces were no longer available and therefore priceless treasures. The Candyland preschool game was headed for the garage sale ("Too boring," Ginny said), but Mousetrap, Lie Detector, Yahtzee, Clue, Life, and Chutes and Ladders were headed for Lindsay's. Monopoly, Scrabble, and a chess and checker set would be on the moving van along with ten of the thirty or so jigsaw puzzles.

The bookcases held even more irreplaceable riches. Lindsay's personal take-home pile became larger and larger as the books that missed the "top ten most special" in each category, (illustrated picture books, first readers, first chapter books, young readers, mystery, history, science, travel, book group fiction, book group non-fiction, cookbooks, sewing, and biography), but ones Ginny could not bear to part with, were piled by the door with a promise of safe-keeping at Lindsay's and division among siblings or grandchildren at some point in the future.

"Maybe we should just designate one section of our basement for all their stuff," Lindsay said to Mo that evening in bed. "She really isn't ready to part with so many things, no matter what she says. And Dad's just as bad…he's making piles of his tools to give to each of us."

"It's okay, honey," Mo consoled his wife. "Whatever it takes to get them out. Once they get away from it all and enjoy their freedom from stuff, then they won't care as much," Mo kissed her cheek. "It'll be okay. Just pile it in the basement beside my parents' stuff that we still haven't dealt with. Then someday we'll have the mother of all garage sales."

"You should see the pile in the garage for *their* sale. Already. I'm going to make Robert and Sophie start helping. And I think we should make Pam come home, too. It's a good lesson for us all to quit collecting stuff right now."

"Well, good luck with that," Mo thought of the difficulty of getting his own brother to fly home from the mid-West when his parents were downsizing. He loved Lindsay's siblings, but none were as involved in their parents' lives as she was, even though her younger brother Robert and his wife Jill and their little daughters, and her next-oldest sister Sophie and her teenage daughters, all lived in town, and they saw one another often. "Just go with the flow, honey," he advised, then rolled over and fell promptly asleep.

But Lindsay did not fall asleep, instead working out a detailed plan that would get the job done, efficiently and promptly.

Chapter Seven

Tess parked in front of the Noonan's home and approached the open, double-wide garage where Lindsay, Ginny, and Frank were busy sorting and marking items for the next morning's garage sale.

"Wow!" she announced upon her arrival. "I'm impressed. This is a lot of stuff!"

Lindsay glanced in her direction. "Grab a marker and some stickers and have at it. We're not even halfway through."

"Welcome, Tess," Ginny approached and gave her daughter's best friend a warm hug. "Thank you for coming to help. I fear the troops are beginning to flag. Especially the commander." She indicated Lindsay with a nod of her head.

"We've been doing this for days," Lindsay paused. "There's no end to it."

Tess returned Ginny's embrace. "Remember my mom's sale? We thought there wouldn't be that much, and then she just kept pulling stuff out of closets at the last minute. I think it's always this way."

"I'm going to bring out some refreshments." Ginny headed into the house. "Tess, what can I get you to drink? There's coffee on, or something cold?"

"Anything cold with caffeine."

"Hey, Tess," Frank called from the back corner of the garage, where he was going through the final boxes. "Need any gardening tools? We're not taking very many with us."

"That means less than thirty," Lindsay said under her breath.

"I can always use new hand clippers, if you have any that actually cut," Tess replied. "Mine are practically rusted shut."

"Here," Frank held out a pair for her. "We have...uh...several."

Lindsay shook her head. Working at a rectangular table they had brought out from the house, she was marking practically new hardback books either fifty cents or one dollar. She tried to keep them in their organizational categories, but it was getting difficult as she ran out of room. She had already marked all her parent's clothing, the kitchen items, the CDs and DVDs. Several boxes of children's clothing were waiting, all of it rejected by her siblings. Her mother had saved one box of her all-time favorites: the infant baptism dresses and Robert's tiny suit, the first crawlers, a few favorite toddler shirts and the Easter outfits. Lindsay's queries regarding what possible use her mother would make of these forty-year-old clothes could make no dent. "I like the colors," is all Ginny would reply. "I'll find a use for them someday."

"What can I do?" Tess inquired helpfully.

"You could pull all the Halloween costumes out of those four boxes over there and hang them on that rolling laundry cart. Then make up some prices for them. I think anything from two to five dollars."

Tess rearranged some skis, a manual typewriter and a box of mason jars to make herself a workspace. "Is the commode going or staying?"

"It's for sale. They'll have all that rehab stuff at the Gardens if it's needed."

"You'd be surprised how many people we've lent that commode to over the years," Frank spoke up from his corner. "It's one of the more handy pieces of medical equipment after surgery. We actually just used it after your mom's fall over the train set. Set it beside the bed and she didn't have to use crutches in the middle of the night to get to the bathroom."

"I wonder. Maybe I should take it for my mom. Or, if I put it outside in summer, would it keep the boys from tracking in dirt every time they have to pee?"

"Take it," Frank said. "We'd be glad to have it stay in the family."

Tess put the adult potty in the driveway, and came back to the costumes. First out was a lovely Little Red Riding Hood cape. "This is nice," Tess announced as she swung the cape around her shoulders and did a twirl. She saw the accompanying basket in the box and hooked it over her arm, instantly appearing as if she were walking through the woods to visit her grandmother. "Really nice." She admired the well-sewn cape and stuck a four dollar sticker on it, hooking the basket on the hanger, also. Next out was a black, stuffed horse's head, complete with a white yarn mane and a blaze along its nose. "I remember this one!" She pulled the horse's neck over her head, admiring the fit and how she had good vision out the horses' mouth. "Your mom's incredible," her voice was muffled.

"If you try them all on, you're going to be here all night," Lindsay advised wearily.

Ginny arrived as Tess was attaching the horse's head to a hanger with safety pins.

"That was the year Lindsay was so horse crazy," Ginny said, putting down her tray of drinks and chocolate chip cookies. "It always wobbled a little at a certain angle, though."

"And look at this one!" Tess exclaimed as she pulled out a toddler penguin suit. "Oh, my goodness. I have to have this one."

"You're really not helping," Lindsay said dryly. "We've already been through them, and half are in my pile to take home and save for the great-grandchildren twenty years from now."

"There will be more babies before you know it," her mother corrected her. "Gwen is seventeen. In ten years she could be married with children."

Tess held up a green, fringed shirt with tan patches and brown, felt shoe covers with bells on the toes. "What's this one?" She jingled the bells merrily.

"Peter Pan. One of my first attempts."

"Tinker Bell is probably right beneath. Do you think you could just hang and mark?" Lindsay asked with some impatience.

"Sorry. But really, Ginny, they are lovely. I'd blocked from my memory those Halloweens when Lindsay was dressed to the nines and I had on a paper bag with holes cut out for eyes. Didn't I go as the Marlboro man one year...with just a cowboy hat on my head and wearing my winter coat?"

"I think that was the year Lindsay used the horse costume. That was your mother's idea, as I recall. I'm sure I have a picture. Let me go look."

"NO!" Lindsay took the bait. "No one's allowed to leave the garage until we finish this. People will start showing up at seven a.m. no matter what the signs say."

"I was only teasing you, darling. Here, I think you need some sugar." Ginny brought the cookie plate to her daughter. "Just don't get chocolate on the books."

Lindsay brought a gooey chocolate chip oatmeal cookie to her lips, the calming mantra her therapist had suggested coming to mind: "Breathe and remember, breathe and remember." Supposedly the happy memories attached to all the stuff would miraculously overwhelm and calm her feelings of panic and despair. Lindsay paused and took several deep breaths, then observed Tess with a white bunny hat on her head, stretching to see herself in the old wall mirror that was also going out. The mantra didn't really seem to be working.

"How much for the mirror?" Tess inquired. "It would look great in my front hallway by the hat rack."

"It's yours," Frank boomed from his work station. "Just be careful, the wire's a little loose on the back. Actually, put it over on my workbench and I'll fix it for you before you leave."

"No, no, don't worry about it. I can tighten it up at home." Tess had felt Lindsay's eyes boring through her. "I'll stick it out there on the commode, and then I'm going to finish these costumes and move on to…what's next?"

"The old electronics, I think," Lindsay answered. "I wanted to take them all to a recycler, but Dad swears people will want them and will fix them up. They're not technically broken, but, you know. Out-of-date."

"A toaster is a toaster," her father declared. "Someone will make good use of it. And the electric can opener, and the 1960 electric frying pan, and the wok. They're all in good condition."

"What are these?" Tess walked to the shelf beneath the garage window, where four urns rested.

"I think those are the remains of the four dogs of my childhood," Lindsay said.

"You never buried them? They just sit here?"

"I think of them fondly whenever I see them," Ginny said.

"Could be worse," Lindsay said to Tess in a low voice. "She would have put our grandparents there if given half a chance."

"I heard that!" Ginny retorted. "Would have saved a lot of money, that's all I'll say."

Saturday morning, the sun burst through a light mist. Lindsay arrived early, having set out more Garage Sale signs on her way. Her dad was setting up the pay table, her mom organizing the cash in the old-fashioned cash drawer. Lindsay tried to observe her parents with an impartial eye. Were they okay doing this? She had seen whole ranges of emotion during the past three weeks, but in the end, it seemed the pendulum had landed on the "glad to be doing this" end

40

of the scale. The interior of their home was taking on its original spacious qualities as some of the furniture had gone to various family members, and nearly all the clutter had been sorted, packed, tossed, given away, or set out for sale. There had been one last minute glitch over the old Lionel train set. Lindsay had been sure her father would be ready to pass it on to one of the grandchildren, but instead it was packed up, along with nearly 20 boxes of accessories, to move. "I've always had a Christmas train," is all her father would say. "I'm not stopping now."

Cars cruised down the street, neighbors wandered by. By nine o'clock business was brisk. Lindsay replaced her parents at the cash table, as they had gotten into such long conversations with each person that the line snaked around the side of the house to cash out. Tess arrived and spelled her a bit. By afternoon, Lindsay's older sister Sophie, along with her two daughters, Gwen and Kara, and her younger brother Robert, wife Jill, and their little girls, had all been by to help.

"Can I have this?" Four-year-old Francie held up a stuffed bunny nearly as tall as she.

"Can you pay for it? The give aways were last weekend," Frank teased his youngest grandchild.

"No!" her father Robert answered from across the driveway. "We're not taking anything else."

Sunday went the same as Saturday, brisk business all day. They cut all the prices by mid-afternoon, and that spurred a last buying spree in the neighborhood. Lindsay had arranged for a Goodwill truck to come Monday morning and haul off whatever wasn't taken, and there was still plenty to send with them. But her parents had made over a thousand dollars, and that seemed to please them.

Now they just had to finish repairs to the house, prepare to put it on the market, and wait for an opening at Lakeview Gardens.

Chapter Eight

Remarkably, just as Frank was putting the final touches on some outside painting on a sunny mid-October day, a three-bedroom, first-floor apartment opened up at the Gardens. It didn't have the same majestic panorama as the apartments on the top floor, but there was a partial lake view, and gardens out the living room and master bedroom windows. "There's no guarantee when a top-floor will become available," Iris had said, encouraging them to move forward. "And if you move in, you'll have first choice of any apartments that become available over new residents from the outside."

Ginny and Frank had decided to take it. Living in their big barren house, trying to keep it clean and not fill it up again, was making Ginny feel anxious and depressed. If they were going to move, let's get on with it, she felt. They were using an old friend as their realtor, ready to list the house as soon as an apartment became available. With the Seattle housing market still in a slump, they weren't sure how long their house would take to sell. They could manage both places for a while, and would try to set a fair price.

Lindsay accompanied them for the walk-through.

"I'm so glad you could make it today," Iris opened the apartment door with a flourish. "The first floor apartments are actually in rather high demand. Close to parking, don't have to wait for the elevator to come and go. I have several people on the waiting list, so I won't be able to hold it for you for long."

The smell of new paint greeted them, the light wall color and new cream carpeting creating the feeling of spaciousness and light.

42

"It's so wonderful, Mom," Lindsay exclaimed. "Most of your living room furniture is going to fit in here, and the dining set in the alcove, it's going to feel just like home." They toured the bedrooms, Lindsay and Frank using a measuring tape to confirm that the beds, dressers, and even the bedside tables would fit. The built-in storage in the hallway closet looked ready to receive forty years of photos, and the wardrobe in the extra bedroom would house the Lionel train boxes.

Ginny looked around. Now that they had jettisoned so much from their own house, it was a little easier to see how they would fit into this new space. She could do it. She glanced at Frank. Since the garage sale, he had seemed more certain that they were doing the right thing, moving while they were young enough to adjust and make new friends. She knew he would miss his garage junk, but there was a workshop in the building for the residents, right beside the small potting shed. They could make it work, Ginny was sure of it. Whenever she had a memory glitch, it reinforced her determination that this was the right move. If she kept getting worse, Frank would need some help.

"And here's the kitchen," Iris said brightly, turning on the overhead lights. "So much storage space in this configuration. A nearly new refrigerator, and new flooring."

Ginny admired the worktop laminate, an off-white pattern that kept with the space-and-light enhancing theme throughout the apartment. There was lots of counter space for the coffee maker and toaster oven; a microwave was tucked in nicely below the upper cupboards. Attractive under-the-cabinet lighting added to the glow of the room. Ginny approached the stove and automatically turned on the right front burner and held her hand over the coil, wondering if it would be fast or slow to heat.

"Oh," Iris said, "the stoves aren't plugged in."

"Excuse me?" Ginny turned.

"Liability. There's no cooking in the apartments other than the microwaves, toasters and coffeemakers. You can have all your meals in the dining room if you like. There's really no reason to have a stove at all. We put them in to make it look homey. You'd be surprised what some people store in the ovens!" She smiled reassuringly.

Frank glanced at his daughter, whose face had paled considerably.

"I can't possibly live somewhere where I can't cook and bake," Ginny stated simply. She turned to her husband and daughter. "Did you know about this?"

"No," Lindsay lied.

"I had no idea," Frank replied dramatically, although he'd had a pretty good inkling from the research he'd done on senior living in general.

"But, Mom, you can come and bake at my house. Any time you want," Lindsay offered feebly, too little, too late.

"And we have many cooking events in the activity center. That stove works," Iris chirped brightly, still missing the immensity of the problem. "You can use it whenever an activity isn't scheduled."

"Well, I think we're done here, Frank. Let's go."

"But, Mom, wait. Wait. We'll figure it out...." Lindsay burst into tears.

Ginny turned to her daughter, a betrayed sadness in her voice. "I can't possibly live anywhere where I can't cook. It's as simple as that." Ginny walked out the door.

"Dad, what can we do? We've signed the papers. The house goes on the market tomorrow!" Lindsay fumbled in her purse for tissues, tears streaming down her face.

"Nothing's done that can't be undone," Frank put his arm around his daughter. "Moving was a tough sell in the first place, even though your mom acted like she wanted to do it. I'm not bringing her here if she's going to be unhappy."

"Most of our residents quickly get used to the arrangements," Iris tried to catch up in the conversation. "They look forward to seeing their friends at meal time."

"I'll see you in the car," Frank said to his daughter, and left to catch up with his wife.

Ginny sat stiffly in the front seat.

Frank settled himself behind the wheel, then reached over and took her hand.

"I'm sorry. I didn't know. To be honest, I'm not surprised, but when I saw there was a stove there on our first walk-through, I figured it worked. I never thought they'd put one in just for show."

A tear slid down Ginny's cheek. "I would have done it, really. I didn't want to, but I would have gone for you. But not now."

"I understand." He squeezed her hand, then started the car to get the heater going while they waited for Lindsay. "Well, on the bright side, the house is all cleaned out. We won't know what to do with all the room."

Ginny smiled grimly. "We'll just have to start over, I suppose. And I want my furniture back."

"I guess I'll round up my tools. Hopefully the kids haven't hocked them yet."

Chapter Nine

For the rest of October, a slow procession of large vehicles arrived at the house, carting furniture back in, like busy ants storing up for winter: a piece here, a piece there, until the house was nearly back together. Only the clutter was missing, and Ginny decided she didn't miss that at all.

She met each group of relatives and movers with a plate of homemade cookies at the door, as if to prove she certainly could not exist without her oven.

On the day before Halloween, Frank was headed to the hardware store to pick up some wire and plywood for the display he was working on to surprise his grandchildren. The light ahead had changed to red, and he slowed to a stop in the Jeep, thinking about his shopping list when suddenly the Volvo that was following behind him bumped the Jeep quite sharply.

Frank looked in his rear view mirror to see the face of a teenage boy. Motioning to pull off onto the nearby side street, the Volvo followed him slowly.

Frank hopped out, ready to be angry at the inattentiveness of the teen who was extricating himself from the car. "I'm so sorry!" the boy apologized profusely, seeming distraught, before Frank could get out a word.

A petite older woman sat in the passenger seat of the Volvo. "Is your passenger all right?" Frank asked with concern, thankful the airbags had not deployed.

"I think so. She's my grandmother. It startled her, is all. I'm so sorry. I looked away because she was coughing so hard, I thought she was choking. I didn't see the light change. We're going to the doctor."

Frank figured the boy couldn't have been more than sixteen. "Been driving long?"

"Just got my license. My parents are going to kill me. I've been so careful, but...."

At this point the grandmother emerged from the car, dressed for an outing, including make-up, hat and jewelry. "Hello!" she said brightly.

"Are you sure you're all right?" Frank approached her, trying to determine why she looked a little odd.

"You'll have to excuse me, I don't have my teeth in!" She gave a toothless grin, followed by a wracking cough.

"That's quite a cough you've got there. If you're sure you're all right, we'll just exchange information and you can be on your way."

Another coughing spell spewed forth before she managed, "My daughter and son-in-law both work, so they asked Billie to take me to the doctor. I really hate to go out right now until I get my new teeth. They're going to attach all the uppers to my back molars, that's all I've got left up there."

Frank had his wallet out as he listened, patting his pockets for a pen and piece of paper.

"Yup, I lost my teeth but I got my mind back! I got the better of that trade for sure!" The toothless wonder continued with more smiles and giggles again followed by the horrendous cough.

Frank took a step back, hoping to avoid the spray.

"Grandma, don't start on it!" The young boy had found a pen and old gas receipt in his car, and tore the slip in half and offered it to Frank, then began copying down his own insurance information.

"People need to know! You youngsters don't understand what it's like to lose your memory and then get it back."

He had been half listening, but now Frank's full attention riveted to the woman.

"What's that, now?"

"My teeth were causing my memory loss! My denture cream. Something about the ingredients depleting something in your body you need and they discovered it relates to memory loss. A week after I quit using my cream, I was good as new! They were about to ship me off to an old folks' home, and now I'm still in my own place!" Another round of coughing followed this pronouncement.

"Grandma—they weren't shipping you off—"

"Is that true? What she says about the denture cream?" Frank turned to the boy again, thinking of Ginny's morning ritual of carefully spreading the cream on her dentures.

"Oh, yeah, that's true. My mom saw the tiniest article about it in the paper, and took it to Grandma's doctor. You could probably look up the article, it was about six weeks ago, right, Grandma?"

"It was September 18, I'll never forget that date as long as I live." The coughing started again and the boy reached in the car and brought out a water bottle. She took a good swig, nearly choked, but finally caught her breath. "Course if I don't get over this pneumonia, I may die anyway. But at least I've got my mind back!" She paused for a breath before continuing. "Supposedly you have to use more than the prescribed amount, but some people must be more susceptible, my daughter said, because I was always careful about it. Except when they were slipping around and I needed more!"

Frank sized up the diminutive woman, chugging more water, then giving her lips a wipe on her silky sleeve. The boy had grown ashen as he examined the damage to the grill of his parent's newish Volvo.

"Listen, there's not much damage on mine." Frank tried to contain his excitement over the denture cream possibilities. "Let's just forget about it. You go along and get your grandma to the doctor."

"Are you sure?"

48

"Yes. Here's my phone number. You give me your parents' and I'll call them tonight so they know it's all okay. Actually, I'd like to talk to your mom about that memory thing."

Ginny, at the sink washing baking pans, startled when her husband rushed through the back door and attacked the keyboard at the kitchen computer.

"Frank? What is it? What's happened? You were barely gone twenty minutes. What's wrong?" She began to feel frightened at his hurried movements and intense concentration on the screen until she saw the smile spreading across his face.

"You're going to look beautiful without your dentures."

"What are you talking about?"

"Come and see." Frank let his wife take his seat at the computer, and watched lovingly as the look on her face changed from concern, to surprise, to wonder.

"So that's it?" Lindsay's mother-in-law Joan sat across from Ginny at the breakfast table in Ginny's kitchen. "It was the denture cream?"

"Yup. Too much zinc can cause a loss of copper in your system, and that can lead to memory loss and other problems."

"And to find out because that young man was taking his grandmother to the doctor and slammed into Frank, how wonderful is that?"

"I know. Otherwise we would never have known. Never even saw that article in the paper. You'd think someone would have made a bigger deal about it, but I guess it didn't affect everyone the same way. I feel so fortunate we discovered it."

"You must have been terribly worried. I never noticed you having any lapses."

"It was so inconsistent, is the thing. But the worst was the day I forgot Alex at Nordstrom's. Really, that's the day I decided we had to move. Thank goodness those stoves at Lakeview Gardens weren't plugged in...think if we'd sold the house!"

Joan nodded in agreement, then her head sagged and she burst into tears.

"Joan, what is it? What's happened?" Ginny couldn't imagine what had so upset her friend.

"Our apartments are going condo."

"Oh, no." Ginny was relieved, as this did not seem too serious. "Aren't they offering you a buy-in?"

"Paul's furious. He'll have no part of it. He can't stand homeowner's associations. He says they'll bleed us dry, always raising the monthly maintenance rates. He started looking for houses."

Ginny found a box of tissues and plopped them on the table as Joan continued, wiping her eyes.

"But I don't want to have a house again. I've been so happy in the apartment. It's so simple and clean. And easy. We can lock it and go when we travel. I don't want the responsibility of homeownership. All those years I worked and kept up a house and took care of the boys. And watered the plants and the mowed the lawn, and washed windows and cleaned carpets. When Paul had his own church, before he started teaching, he was so busy, I had to do everything. I love our life now. No gardening. No maintenance. If something doesn't work, we call the manager, they come the same day and fix it."

Ginny marveled at the difference between people. She loved Joan dearly, but contemplating life at Lakeview Gardens without her flower beds and garden had been a depressing thought. Simple and easy for Joan was boring and claustrophobic to Ginny. With Frank being so handy, household repairs were usually a snap, whereas Paul was often the recipient of frequent teasing over his hesitancy to even pick up a screwdriver. Yet although his career had been as a parish pastor and then teaching Old Testament at a local college, the man had a gift for finance where she and Frank struggled to find the happy medium between money under the mattress and too-good-to-be-true investments that risked everything. Mush the two men together, and Paul and Frank would make the perfect husband, Ginny reasoned thoughtfully.

Continuing to observe the weeping Joan, it was as if the audio portion had been turned off in Ginny's mind. An odd feeling came over her, as a wild idea slowly took shape. But could it work? Could it possibly work?

A week later, Lindsay noted the Walker & Sons contractor's truck in the driveway as she arrived unannounced at her parents' house.

"What's Dad up to now?" She kissed her mom on the cheek as she plunked her purse down on the kitchen table.

"Getting some estimates. We're fixing up the old bathroom upstairs."

"Whatever for?"

"Resale value, I guess. You know, when your father gets an idea in his head. Only having one full bath up there was a mark against us before."

Lindsay didn't like the funny tone in her mother's voice. Something was up. Something was definitely up. She observed her mom with a keen eye, trying to discern the truth.

Ginny flashed her a happy smile and opened a tin on the counter. "Cookie?"

Chapter Ten

"They're doing what?" Lindsay stood dumbfounded in the doorway. Her husband Mo had arrived home first and already had dinner reheating in the oven. He had been carefully planning how to break the news to his wife, but in the end had simply blurted it out.

"They're moving in together. Your parents invited mine to live with them. What a gracious gesture, don't you think? Kills several birds with a couple of stones."

Lindsay sank into a kitchen chair and took the cold glass of water her husband offered. Now it all made sense. "That's why they're remodeling the upstairs."

"Yup. Breaking through the wall and making a big master bedroom and sitting room out of the two bedrooms, and then enlarging the bath on that end of the hall, too."

"Why didn't they just tell me?"

"My parents wanted to tell me first. Who knows why. But what a great solution. The house was too big for your folks. And mine didn't really want to get a new house, no matter how small. It's perfect."

"I guess so." A hundred ways that it was NOT perfect were racing through Lindsay's mind. She had been blessed with such wonderful parents and in-laws, but what if they drove each other crazy in such close quarters? What if they all four got sick? What if something happened to the house? What if they fought over repairs, or the cooking, or *anything*, and it ruined their friendship? What if Mo's parents convinced her parents to travel more? What if they were never home? And could never babysit? What if they went away for the holidays?

Slowly, reason began to crowd out her doubts. Due to the cramped quarters of Paul and Joan's apartment, they already spent all the holidays at her parents', so nothing would change there. And her mother really did not enjoy travel. Or hadn't so far.

Lindsay turned the news over and over in her mind, and finally went out on the front porch to call Tess.

"I think it's a great idea," Tess chimed in, as she browned ground turkey in a frying pan to make spaghetti sauce for dinner. "It's brilliant, really. All the birds in one nest. Like the scene from Charlie and the Chocolate Factory."

"Mo loves that scene, all four grandparents in the four-poster bed together. But don't forget Charlie's mom, the harried daughter, trying to take care of them all. Everyone forgets that part."

"You're so dramatic. This is a great resolution. You've got your three sibs, Mo, and Mo's brother to help. Think of my situation….just me and my far away brothers to take care of my mom. And you know how much help they are."

"I know," Lindsay could hear Mo calling the kids to dinner. "I'm not complaining. I'm…I'm pre-complaining. I'm putting it out there that there's a possibility for trouble, that's all."

"Fine. I'll mark on my calendar that today, November 20, 2009, at 6:10 p.m., you reserved the rest of your life for future trouble. Okay?"

"Good enough. Thank you for recognizing my anxiety. Talk to you later."

Lindsay smiled. That was the wonderful thing about Tess; she could lampoon all fears with a single, sharp, spear of sarcasm.

Chapter Eleven

Six days later, Thanksgiving dinner was in full swing at the Noonan's when Paul and Joan excused themselves from the extended table around which they had all gathered to take a call from their younger son and his partner, who lived in Chicago. They returned to the table, Joan's face flushed with excitement.

"They're getting married! December 12 in Boston. A last-minute cancellation opened up a spot at their venue! Of course, your whole family is invited!" Joan radiated happiness.

"Massachusetts in December? I thought they had a date for next fall," Ginny asked curiously.

"They did, but Joseph said they've waited so long, they'd rather have a simpler ceremony now. You never know if the marriage equality laws are going to hold, and they've waited long enough…ten years," Joan answered, her voice choking a bit.

"Will you perform the ceremony?" Frank asked Paul.

"Yes. I'm pleased they asked me."

"We better get started on airline tickets," Mo said, ever the practical one, as he reached for another helping of stuffing and gravy. "Hopefully there might be some good deals before the Christmas rush."

"Maybe," Ginny mumbled, attempting enthusiasm for holiday travel which she ordinarily dreaded.

A few days later, Lindsay dropped by her parents' house after dinner, returning the containers she had borrowed to take home leftover turkey and sides. "So," she slipped into a chair across from her mom, who was cutting quilt squares on the dining room table, "will you and Dad go?"

"I don't know, honey. It's a long way for a weekend. Of course we love Joseph, and Tristan is perfectly wonderful. But Seattle to Boston...."

"Well," Lindsay began slowly. "If you and Dad don't mind skipping it, what would you think about keeping the kids?"

"Your kids?" Ginny brightened at this unexpected offer. "Of course, we'd be glad to do that for you."

"What about more kids? Like, all the kids."

"Which 'all' the kids?"

"Jill and Sophie and I have been talking. We all want to go, but it's expensive. None of us have been to Boston before. If we could leave the grandkids with you, it would be cheaper and a little sibling vacation for us. Pam's flying up from D.C., we'd all be there."

"All seven grandkids? For what, two or three nights?"

"Maybe four. We'd go Friday, and take Monday off so we could sightsee a little bit. Home Tuesday. Like you said, it's a long way to go for a weekend."

"I'll have to think about it," Ginny said uncertainly. "And ask your father. Maybe he wants to go."

"I checked with Dad. He's fine with it if you are. Sophie's girls will help: Gwen can drive herself and Kara around, Sophie will let them bring the car. You know my Amelia and Carol won't be any trouble. And Alex will help you entertain Mara and Francie."

"What about all their activities and things?"

"Covered. Like I said, Gwen and Kara will take care of themselves. I'll arrange rides for Amelia and Carol. That just leaves the three youngest."

Alex and the hurricanes, Ginny thought of Frank's fond nickname for the little girls. Ginny studied her daughter, who had obviously spent the last forty-eight hours on the phone with her siblings and sister-in-law.

"And the only big event that weekend will be their soccer games," Lindsay continued her pitch. "The Seattle City Tournament will have started. So the oldest four will probably have matches. But you won't even have to go; like I said, transportation is already taken care of. It really impacts laundry more than anything else. Socks and uniforms and all that. The kids are super responsible for their stuff."

From the state of her adult children's homes, Ginny knew Lindsay's last statement was not even in the ballpark of partial truth, much less whole truth. But still, it was only for a weekend. And when she balanced the effort to travel to Boston for two or three nights versus taking care of the grandkids in her own home, staying won hands down. Besides, it *would* be wonderful for the adult siblings to have a weekend together. The Noonan and Rogers families had been close for years. This was a major life event for Paul and Joan, to finally have both sons married. Ginny decided she could cheerfully do her part to make it a memorable weekend for all.

The troops staggered in on Thursday evening with a mountain of luggage, arriving damp and chilled after being participants in or observers of the scheduled soccer matches, except for little Francie and Mara who had come over directly after school to get settled before the big kids arrived. With an early Friday morning departure for the Boston-bound parents, it had been decided it made more sense to have the kids spend an extra night with their grandparents rather than have all the fuss of an early drop-off at the crack of dawn.

Ginny welcomed each group at the door, separating them from their wet clothing and sending the soaked uniforms and socks straight to the washer. The City Tournament for recreation youth soccer teams in Seattle was a time-honored tradition of rather grueling matches for each age level beyond mid-elementary school, ending with finals right before Christmas. The brackets were a nightmare for any kind of family holiday event scheduling…you didn't know until you won or lost the game you were actually playing where and when your next game might be, and games were all over the city. Luckily, the muddy fields of her own children's soccer years had changed to turf for her grandkids, so mud was less of a factor. But there had been many times when she was still standing on a soccer field sideline, soaked and frozen, on the Saturday before Christmas, wondering what on earth she was doing there when there was so much to be done at home.

Friday morning went well, getting all the children dropped off at various schools, and Ginny was encouraged. She and Frank picked up four-year-old Francie at lunch time, as her pre-school/daycare was beginning a week of school conferences. "It's starting at pre-school now?" Ginny murmured to her husband as she hopped out of the car to retrieve their granddaughter.

Dinner went well, as both daughters and daughter-in-law had brought a wide-range of favorite foods covering the vegan, vegetarian, lactose-intolerant and gluten free preferences of the children. Gwen, the oldest, was permitted to go to the movies with her boyfriend; Kara went to the mall with some friends; and the rest of them settled in to watch movies at home.

The first difficulty on Saturday was a last-minute change in the soccer schedule: Gwen and Kara's games ended up being at the same time on different sides of the city, and it took Kara some time to find an alternate ride. Ginny's hope that perhaps at least one of the four children's teams would have been washed out of the tournament by now were dashed, as all four were bravely fighting their way through the losers' brackets, which was the worst possible path to winning the first place trophy, and involved games every other day.

But they survived Saturday and by evening there were mounds of soccer gear drying everywhere. Ginny had wanted to take the children to church on Sunday morning, but the sheer effort of cajoling, insisting, bribing and guilting seemed too much, and instead they stayed in their pajamas until ten and then had a lovely brunch, with each guest managing to find one or two foods that they would eat.

After lunch Ginny and Frank took the three youngest, Robert and Jill's little girls Mara and Francie, and Lindsay and Mo's youngest, Alex, shopping. Hopes of a family picture with Santa had also been dashed; the teenagers all had plans of their own. Alex's older sisters, Amelia and Carol, at 14 and 12, caught between the two age groups, were allowed to go with their older cousins for the afternoon, after promising to check-in every hour as to their whereabouts.

Ginny and Frank took the youngest three to the packed mall to see the decorations, but the parking was terrible and Ginny was tired from the effort before they even made it through the door. Ginny and Frank only had one moment of panic when they momentarily lost the little girls, who, upon entering the toy store, had caught sight of the Lego section and disappeared down an aisle unseen by their grandparents. Alex solved the problem by simply yelling their names at the top of his seven-year-old lungs which was very effective and reunited the family in no time. Each girl's hand was then firmly in the grasp of a grandparent for the rest of the outing.

After dinner the kids all talked to their parents and Ginny and Frank heard all about the wedding from Paul and Joan. Everyone on the East Coast sounded relaxed and happy, Ginny noticed, reminding herself there was no point in being jealous since she knew full well what she was getting into when she agreed to keep the children.

Sunday evening was spent trying to organize the soccer uniforms—shorts, tights, light and dark jerseys, light and dark socks, shin guards, shoes, water bottles, sweats and warm hats—and get it all into the proper soccer bags in preparation for Monday night's games, as well as checking on homework, doing twenty-minutes of reading with Alex and Mara and signing off on their charts, finding all backpacks and gear, and packing lunches for the morning. The older girls were a wonderful help, as their mothers had promised, but it was still a level of chaos Ginny had forgotten about. She and Frank had raised four children who all did sports, but it somehow seemed simpler back then.

On Monday morning, Ginny and Frank made the drop-off rounds to the various schools and then crawled back in bed.

"How many hours until they're home?" Ginny asked.

"A little over twenty-four."

"I'll never make it."

"Sure you will. We just have to feed them now. The big ones will have their soccer matches and homework tonight, and the little ones can watch TV."

"Should we set the alarm to make sure we wake up to go get Francie?" Ginny asked, her eyes already heavy and the blankets pulled up over her clothes.

"I guess so."

But it wasn't the alarm that woke them, but rather the insistent ringing of their cell phones. Frank had accidently set the bedside alarm clock for midnight instead of noon. It was 12:35 and little Francie was sitting in the office at the preschool waiting for them, their son Robert informed his father when Frank finally answered his cell phone. "I was getting ready to call the police and have them break down the door, Dad. You really scared us."

"Oh, for heaven's sakes, we went back to bed, we were tired. I guess we didn't hear the house phone. We're up. Your mother's already out the door."

"Okay. Call us when she gets Francie home."

"Fine, but everything's okay. Gotta go!"

Little Francie was none the worse for wear for her forty-five minute wait in the office. Ginny apologized profusely to the staff, who all nodded understandably when she said they'd been babysitting seven grandchildren over a long weekend and had simply fallen into bed nearly comatose once the kids were all delivered to school.

Ginny stopped at Baskin-Robbins and treated Francie to a cone with sprinkles on their way home.

Francie studied her grandmother seriously across the table as she licked her cone. "Why didn't you go to Boston, Noni?"

"I thought it would be more fun to spend the weekend with you," Ginny answered honestly.

"I'm glad," Francie said with a heart-melting grin, popping the rest of her cone in her mouth happily.

They decided to buy Frank a pint of Rocky Road, his favorite, and then headed home to play games until the rest of the crowd arrived after school.

"I love you, Noni," Francie gave her grandmother an unexpected hug as she was released from her car seat. "I wasn't worried. I knew you'd come for me."

"I'm glad you know Papa and I would never forget you. I'm sorry we fell back asleep so hard. You kids are wearing us out!" Ginny yawned to make her point. "Let's go get some lunch."

"Can I have more ice cream?" Francie's eyes lit up.

"No. But I think there might be some cookies left for snack time later this afternoon. We'll see." She gathered Francie's precious morning artwork, grabbed her purse, took the little hand in hers, and led the way to the front door, where Frank was waiting with a smile.

Chapter Twelve

"I feel like baking," Ginny said after several days of recovery from their weekend of babysitting.

"You always feel like baking," Frank replied, folding the front page of the newspaper neatly and returning it to the other sections piled on the table.

"No, I mean *really* baking."

"Christmas is right around the corner. You always bake a lot then."

"I mean nutritious baking. I'm thinking of something that tastes good, but is healthy. Like a breakfast cookie."

"For the kids?"

"No. I think I'll bake for Tent City. I know a one-time thing is only a one-time thing, but still." Ginny pondered a little longer. "I know. I could start baking breakfast cookies now, and then, on Christmas morning, we could deliver them. The kids aren't coming here till noon. What do you think of that?"

"Okay, I guess. But I was looking forward to being in my pajamas that morning."

"You can be in your pajamas any morning you want to."

"Okay, okay. Guilt bomb received and acknowledged," Frank fake saluted his wife.

"I didn't mean it like that. It would be...kind of a Santa thing to do."

"Okay, I'm in."

Ginny was still figuring out a plan in her head. "Maybe I'll do a cookie recipe, but make them like brownies. That would save some time. Breakfast squares. Or bars. Something. Chocolate chip oatmeal raisin. I should probably skip the nuts. You never know about allergies. I'll freeze them individually in paper wrapping. Minimize the plastic and waste."

"Sounds good." Frank's attention had wandered as he thought about his day.

"Two each for Christmas Day and the day after."

"Uh-huh." Frank got up from the dining room table and took his cereal bowl to the sink.

"So that's four hundred. Thirty-four dozen. Seventeen batches. I think that's doable."

"What?" Frank backtracked. "Four hundred squares?"

"I said I felt like baking. I'll get the kids to help. Maybe use the church kitchen for some of it; that would make it go faster. Big pans, big oven."

Frank took in his wife, now starting a list, head bent over a page of notebook paper and pen poised as she computed ingredients and amounts.

She paused and looked at him happily. "I love Christmas."

Chapter Thirteen

Frank and Ginny settled down on the couch in front of the tree the night before Christmas Eve. The packages were wrapped, the tree was adorned with lights and ornaments, the baking was done. Frank's Christmas train was running around the oval track beneath the tree, its clickety-clack a part of the background noise of every Christmas they had spent together. Nine o'clock and quiet had fallen over the house and neighborhood.

"My favorite time of the holiday, right now," Ginny sighed.

"Not opening presents?" Frank teased, knowing the toll the chaos took on his wife.

"What about you?"

"I like it now, too. It's calm and peaceful."

They sat silently for a few minutes.

"It could be our last Christmas alone, you know," Frank finally said. "Going forward, we'll have Paul and Joan here."

"I know, I've thought about that. But I won't mind, I don't think. Aren't we fortunate to have such good friends in the family? How lucky we are, that our kid would fall in love with theirs?"

"You're sure there was no help on that from you and Joan?"

"None, I swear. When they started dating, I wasn't sure they'd stick with each other. Quite a few differences."

"I liked Mo right from the start. Good grades and a great foul shot. It was always fun watching him play."

"Haven't you been surprised their girls haven't taken to basketball? I suppose there's still a chance with Alex, but you'd think, since both Lindsay and Mo played in high school, their kids would be champs."

"Doesn't always work that way." They sat silently again.

"You know what we need?" Ginny felt suddenly inspired. "A fire. We should be sitting here in front of a roaring fire." She smiled enchantingly at her husband. "It would be romantic. Who knows what might happen, right here in the living room?"

"Whoa. Where's that coming from?" Frank gave his wife a surprised look.

"I don't know. I guess I was thinking of things we'll never do once we have more people living in the house. Intimacy in the living room seems like it might be out."

"Paul and Joan do travel, you know."

"I know, but once they have keys…. Never mind. I guess it was a silly idea."

"Oh, no, I like it." Frank was already on his feet. "I think there are some pressed logs out back that the kids use in the fire pit. I'll get one."

Ginny pulled the wrapped gifts away from the fireplace, opened the wire screen, pulled out the fire place tools, and went to the kitchen to pour some wine.

Frank arrived with a pressed log and stuck it in the fireplace. The paper wrap caught on the first try, snapping and crackling as it burned quickly. Unfortunately, the smoke was not making slow tendrils up the chimney as it should have been, instead collecting and pouring into the room.

"Shit!" Frank muttered, trying to avoid the heat while blindly reaching inside to find the flue.

"Ginny! Did you open the flue?"

"No," Ginny came through the kitchen door, her cheerfulness falling at the smoking room. "Oh, no. I thought you'd do it. I'm sorry. Can you get it?"

64

"Ouch! Dammit, it's hot in there." Frank pulled his hand back.

"Here," his wife ran to his aid, grabbing the hook tool and dropping to her knees so she could see into the swirl of smoke. The metal hook made contact and she pulled the lever. The first rush of cool air was followed by the smoke slowly changing direction and making its way up the chimney.

"Wait for it," Frank said with a sigh. Sure enough, the nearest smoke detector began to sound.

"I'll go," Ginny said. "You open the doors and windows."

In ten minutes the living room was aired out. The log was burning steadily now, and the room seemed no worse for the experience. Ginny retrieved the glasses of cabernet.

"Mood ruined?" she asked her husband.

"On the contrary. Heart rate already up. No foreplay needed." Frank made his way around the room, closing the windows and curtains.

"Oh, you. Romantic was what I was aiming for, remember?"

He took his place on the couch beside her, sliding an arm behind her shoulders. "It's just right." Kissing her cheek, he noted that her hair smelled a bit like smoke. "Now, where were we?"

"I think I'd just said how romantic a fire would be. Little did I know." She rested her head on his broad shoulder. "One of these days, things will go right the first time. But I'm not holding my breath."

"I think we'll manage." Frank rubbed her shoulder gently. "It's been a long time since we've been out of the bedroom."

"Before Pam was born, I think." Ginny murmured, enjoying her husband's warm embrace and tender kisses. They were unbuttoning clothing a bit awkwardly when a sound out front brought Ginny sharply to the present. She pushed Frank back roughly. "What was that?"

"Nothing. A car door across the street." He planted another kiss in the soft spot of her neck.

"No, listen!" she whispered, as she distinctly heard the voices of Robert, Jill, and the little girls. "Run!" she cried, scrambling to her feet, pulling her shirt together and limping hurriedly to the stairway, a few choice words for her creaky knees on the tip of her tongue. Frank was right on her heels. They had just made the landing when the doorbell rang sharply multiple times, followed by excited knocking, and the sound of a key in the lock.

"Why on earth did we ever give them keys?" Frank muttered, as he pulled himself together and then turned to descend.

"Mom? Dad?" Robert poked his head around the door. "So sorry to barge in. Francie needed a bathroom desperately."

Their youngest granddaughter raced past the stairs to the first floor bathroom. "And we have a surprise!!" she yelled over her shoulder. "Kittens!!"

"Kittens?" Ginny floated down the stairs, a bit breathless, now dressed in her long nightgown and bathrobe thrown over her clothes. "I thought you were waiting till February. Aren't the holidays the worst time to get a new pet?"

"Yes," Jill said, entering the warm entranceway with Mara, "but the shelter is full to overflowing with kittens right now, so they called to ask if we could foster some. But we'll keep them. Look." Jill and Mara opened their coats, revealing two tiny striped kittens cradled there.

Francie came bouncing back from the bathroom, and pulled the smaller kitten from her mother's embrace.

"They're only 5 weeks old, found in a parking lot," Robert informed his parents. "Someone turned them in in the nick of time. They wouldn't have lasted in this cold much longer."

"They're darling," Ginny enthused. "Just don't set them—"

Too late, the girls had put their precious babies on the floor, and

66

after a few seconds of being frozen in place, the kittens had scattered, followed by the shrieking girls. In three hops both tiny creatures found refuge as they jumped into the Christmas tree.

"—down." Ginny sighed.

Frank looked at her. "Let's try to get them before the ornaments—"

Again, too late. As if in slow motion, ornaments began sliding off the tree.

"I'm sorry," Jill said. "I'll get them." She then addressed her daughters sternly. "Girls! Stop! Don't chase them. We talked about this, remember?"

Ginny observed her granddaughters, dancing around the tree in excitement. At least, she thought, we're still only putting non-breakables on the tree.

"Is it smoky in here?" Robert queried, observing the fireplace log burning merrily, the wine glasses on the coffee table, and the couch cushions out of place. "Gosh, I hope we didn't interrupt!" he teased.

"Of course not, darling," Ginny reassured him, ignoring her daughter-in-law's questioning look. "But maybe you could get the pet carrier from your car?" She sank onto the couch and patted the seat beside her. "Now girls, come show me these dear little sweethearts."

Jill shooed the girls toward their grandmother and placed one of the kittens in her lap, noticing as she did her mother-in-law's pants cuff peeking out beneath her nightgown and robe.

Chapter Fourteen

Frank lay on his back in bed the morning after Christmas. It was still dark outside, the sun wouldn't be up till nearly 8:00. Yesterday had been the usual frenzy of grandchild excitement and melt-downs, and the visit to Tent City 12 handing out breakfast bars had left him feeling a little low this morning. Ginny was tucked into her familiar place on his chest.

"What is it, honey?" she asked him after the second sigh. "I can feel you thinking very hard about something."

"Oh, nothing. Well, it was Tent City."

"I know. Pretty tough. Especially to go from that to the exuberance and excess of our own Christmas. No easy answers for homelessness, that's for sure."

"I keep seeing the site, with all the tents and platforms pushed up to the one side. I asked a fellow, and he said the drainage is bad. With that hillside at the back, and then there's not much slope where the tents are set up. It's a bog."

"I did notice the pallets making pathways through the mud."

"He said because it's temporary, they're not allowed to make any changes. But I was thinking. It wouldn't take too much to create a catch basin across the back, at least at the worst point, then route the run-off down one side to the street drain."

"What would it take?" Ginny patted his chest lovingly, encouraging his thoughts.

"Concrete blocks. Some drainage tubing. Screening filters. I'm not sure you'd even have to dig anything...maybe just rearrange some dirt here and there."

"Sounds good. Why don't you do it?"

"Oh, I think if it was that easy, someone would have done it already. There's probably permits, or permissions, or who knows what."

"They only moved onto that site two weeks ago. Wouldn't the owners of the lot, even if it's not being used for anything else right now, be glad not to have a mud hole when Tent City leaves? Wouldn't the City be glad not to have all that silt from the hillside washing down the storm drains in heavy rains?"

"You'd think so. But the obvious is not always the common practice."

Ginny snuggled closer. "Go back and talk to them. See what the guys think. Can't hurt, might help."

Thus the following weekend, Frank gathered up the willing and strong of his family, including oldest daughter Pam, who had arrived from DC for New Year's, and a few friends from church, and, with several truckloads of cement blocks, corrugated HDPE drain pipe, and filter screening for the storm drains, plus a huge load of fruit and healthy snacks that Ginny had contributed for the event, the crew set out to "rearrange" some dirt at the encampment. The many hands of the Tent City campers made quick work of creating a mini-retaining wall that caught the water off the hillside, where it then flowed into the corrugated drain pipe and was carried to the street, through three separate filters before ending in the storm drain. The task of clearing the filters was added to the camp chore list, and by the end of the morning, Frank was fairly certain the collection and drainage system would function properly. A drenching rain over the last half-hour had helped prove the point.

Ginny greeted her wet and muddy family at the door.

"Sometimes a one-time thing can be a two-time thing," she said to Frank, offering him a towel. "Who knew Santa was a groundwater engineer?"

Chapter Fifteen

Three weeks later on a mid-January Saturday morning, Lindsay crouched over a paint tray, dragging her roller through a luscious shade of pale yellow that would soon cover the eggshell tan of her old bedroom. Removing the wall between her room and her sisters' to create a larger master bedroom and a smaller sitting room office had been brilliant. A new door in the hallway now divided the upstairs into two sections. The remodeled bathroom and emptied linen closet were adjacent to the new bedroom and sitting room, creating a small suite. Her parents' bedroom, with its attached bathroom, was at the other end of the hall, as was the fourth bedroom, which had been her brother's, but now served as overnight accommodation for the grandchildren.

Brush in hand, Ginny had been cutting out the corners so that Lindsay could roll the middle of the walls. In paint-blotched dungarees, white shirt and hair tucked up and covered with a bandana, her mother looked ten years younger than her 73 years, Lindsay thought.

"This color is gorgeous," Lindsay said to her mother. "Did you pick it?"

"No, Joan did. It's a little lighter than what's in their apartment."

Lindsay rolled her first stroke up the wall, admiring the wide swath of glistening paint. She loved painting: the feel of the roller pressing on the wall; the sound of the paint as it came off the roller; the newness of the color contrasted with the old; the smell of new paint. She loved all of it.

"Mom, I have to admit, these rooms came out so well, I'd like to move in myself. Just me and my stuff...leave Mo and the kids at our house!"

"I don't think we'd fit a tenth of your possessions in here. The only reason it works is that Paul and Joan had already jettisoned everything and embraced the minimalist life style. I admire that, actually."

"Hard to think of two more opposite couples taking up residence together." Lindsay gave an involuntary shudder at the memory of the amount of her parents' belongings that were unearthed during the house clean-out and garage sale in the fall.

"I think that we complement each other," Ginny said happily. "And really, our fundamental values are right in line. It's only around the edges that we're so different."

Lindsay painted awhile, mulling over her parents and in-laws. She was the luckiest person she knew in that regard, and couldn't have more perfect grandparents for her kids. However, there wasn't much sentimentality on Mo's parents' part. Lindsay did sometimes wish she had more pictures of Mo as a child. She had the yearly obligatory school pictures, and that was about it.

"Mom, aren't you worried about losing your privacy?" Lindsay finally asked.

"Privacy can be boring," Ginny said, starting on a new section of wall. "Don't worry, sweetie. It's going to work out just fine."

Chapter Sixteen

On the first morning after the move, Frank felt ashamedly out of sorts when he discovered Paul, the earliest riser, in his chair at the dining room table with the slightly damp newspaper spread before him. The first hurdle of shared space was obviously going to be who would sit where for breakfast.

"Oh, am I in your seat?" Paul asked, catching the look on Frank's face.

"It doesn't matter," Frank replied.

"Of course it matters," Paul said good-naturedly. "If we're all going to get along, these are the very things we must attend to. Now, where shall Joan and I sit at the table? I had assumed you always took the head spot."

"You're right, I guess Ginny and I take the ends on holidays, and that's when you've been over. We actually sit here beside each other. The light seems good."

"All right. Then Joan and I will sit across from you, does that work?"

"Perfect."

Frank got his bowl of cereal and returned to the table, just as Paul put down the front page of the paper and picked up the sports section. Of course, Frank was in the habit of reading the sports section first, but after the seating discussion, he kept quiet and started in on the hard news. Joan arrived next, followed by Ginny, who, as the last one in, had no paper section to read and, even worse, no puzzle page to work on.

"Who does the puzzles here?" Joan asked, folding the comic pages back and looking for a pen.

"We do them together," Ginny replied.

"Oh. Paul does the crosswords and I do the Jumble and Sudoku. Hmm."

"I think we should consider getting two newspaper subscriptions," Frank said. "That way we can all keep our regular routines." He was still itching to get the sports section in his hands.

"Excellent idea," Paul agreed. "I'll make that first on my To Do list for the day."

In their pre-move discussions, the four had decided how they would share the shopping, dinner preparations, and clean-up. Room had been made in the kitchen for two extra types of cereal, a specialty wheat bread, and in the refrigerator for Paul's beloved whole milk beside Frank and Ginny's non-fat. Ginny had tried to clear a little space on each shelf in the cabinets for any canned or dry food Joan would be bringing, but there wasn't much.

Paul and Joan had brought very little furniture, only the pieces for their bedroom and sitting room, and then a small couch, Joan's rocking chair, and Paul's favorite recliner, which all fit into the living room without too much crowding.

They agreed that Ginny would keep parking in the garage, and the others would play first come, first served with the extra driveway space and street parking.

Ginny retrieved a piece of paper and a pen from the kitchen drawer. "We should take stock, I think. Right now, at the beginning."

"Stock of what?" Frank asked.

"Our health," Ginny replied, with a knowing look at Joan.

"What about it?" Paul said, suspecting a pre-arranged agreement between the two women.

"Well, living together, we should know a little bit about each other's health," Joan said.

"I'm good," said Paul.

"I'm good," said Frank.

"And I know you're good," Paul said, indicating his wife, the nurse, whom he suspected of being the instigator of this exercise.

Joan sighed. "All right. Let's try that again. Let's talk about health and meds, and be honest. This is important if we're going to take care of each other." She took the paper and pen from in front of Ginny and put Paul's name at the top. "You first, buster. Meds and health."

"You already know them. Losartin for blood pressure. Daily multi-vitamin and Vitamin C. And a baby aspirin."

"Good. Eyesight? Hearing?"

"Three pairs of glasses: driving, computer, and reading. And a hearing aid, left ear."

"Anything else?"

"No," Paul said firmly, rather annoyed to go first.

"All right, Frank, how about you?"

"Wait a minute," Ginny interrupted. "What about dietary? Is Paul supposed to be eating differently because of his blood pressure?"

"Sort of low salt," Paul answered.

"What does 'sort of' mean?" Ginny asked.

"We don't put the salt shaker on the table anymore," Joan offered.

"That's not low salt. For as much as you guys eat out, you're probably getting tons more salt than you should."

"Let's move on," Paul suggested, ignoring his wife's head nodding in agreement.

"We can work on that," Ginny said. "Don't worry."

"That's what worries me," Paul said under his breath, as a small smile spread across Joan's face.

Frank was pleased that his wife might have someone else to bug about health decisions. But it was a short-lived feeling, as he bared his medical file: same three pairs of prescription lenses as Paul, no hearing trouble, only taking vitamins, but having a cranky lower back, which had not been helped by moving cement blocks into place at Tent City 12 after Christmas.

"Do you have exercises to do?" Joan inquired innocently.

"Yes."

"Do you do them?" Joan continued politely, as Ginny stared pointedly at her husband.

"Not as often as I should," Frank admitted.

"Would you like to add something, Paul?" Joan turned to her beloved.

"My lower back is killing me some days. Sacroiliac. I'm supposed to do exercise, too."

"Now look how well this is going," Ginny said with a smile. "The two of you can do your exercises together."

"You know, Paul, a new gym just opened up in the neighborhood mall," Frank said. "We could walk over there a couple mornings each week and work out for half an hour. They've even got mats for floor work." Frank relished revealing to Paul how plenty of male retirees walked in one gym door and right out the other on their way to the coffee shop. *Going to the gym* had become men's code in the neighborhood for "getting coffee and a sweet roll."

"Sounds good. It's your turn, girls," Paul said. "Let's hear it."

"I'm in perfect shape and I have my recent medical exams to prove it," Ginny said proudly. "Only need readers—I inherited my mom's good eyesight. My knees aren't great, is all. But I take my vitamins and a baby aspirin every day."

"And we should probably get Frank on low dose aspirin, too," Joan added. "The literature isn't conclusive, but everyone our age takes it. Unless you're having stomach trouble?" she peered at Frank again.

"No stomach trouble. But what about you, Joan?" Frank inquired courteously.

"Trifocals and bad knees is all. An occasional sore hip. I try to walk every day."

"Oh, I do, too," Ginny said. "You'll love it here, so easy to get on the trail or just walk the neighborhood."

"Okay," Joan looked at her list. "That's a good start. Tomorrow we'll take up hobbies and mental health. Meditation has been thoroughly recommended for our age group. Sound good?"

"Great," Paul said, stacking the sports page neatly on the other sections. "I'll go order another newspaper."

"I'm going to check that the downspouts are draining okay," Frank excused himself.

Paul and Frank nearly knocked into each other escaping from the table, both thinking the same thing: the laser-like attention of two wives on their health, eating, and spare-time habits had the horrifying possibility of being much more intense than simply doubling the effect of one spouse's scrutiny.

Even so, the first week of living together went more smoothly than any of them could have imagined. After securing the seating arrangements at the table, the next organizational decision was what to do about keys and glasses. With four vehicles, eight sets of keys, and glasses of various prescription strengths floating around the house, it became evident by the third time Frank had tried to read with Paul's glasses that a system was called for.

They decided on a series of little baskets on top of the four-shelf bookcase inside the front door. Each labeled with either a vehicle or a human name, all associated paraphernalia for each was to be returned to the basket if found in an odd place in the house. They each had one special place where they left their reading glasses when not in use: top of the microwave, top of the TV, top of the CD player on the kitchen counter, and on a shelf of the dining room hutch. After a short discussion about whether it was better to move misplaced items or wait for the owner to remember where they'd been left, they decided to do their aging brains a favor and all pitch in and look out for each other. Thus after the first few days, there had been hardly any "Have you seen my glasses or keys?" questions.

By the second week, the four were truly enjoying their time together, discussing the news, politics, and the comings and goings of their children over breakfast. The morning after Ginny received news of a good friend's stroke, they had a more serious discussion about how they might care for each other in the face of declining health or an unexpected crisis.

"I think the stairs will be the biggest problem," said Paul. "For right now, they're good exercise. But if any mobility trouble arises, we're sunk."

"We can always make the den on this floor into a bedroom," Frank said. "And we can probably get a small walk-in shower in the bathroom here. Might need to go through the wall and take out the kitchen pantry." Frank had already had this plan in his head for some time.

The four sat soberly for a moment, contemplating the host of possible unknowns.

"Prevention is the key," Joan finally said. "Exercise, eat right, good mental health. And it seems like family genes are in our favor all the way around. We're lucky that way."

"Let's simply refuse to age," Ginny said. "The seventies haven't been too bad so far."

"My new goal is to make it to 85 in one piece, right here in this house," Paul quipped. "That's only ten years."

"It could get pretty crowded in that downstairs bedroom," Frank said.

"Last one standing on two legs gets the pie?" Joan asked.

"And the whole upstairs," Ginny murmured.

Chapter Seventeen

Over the next month, the couples settled into an easy routine. They each had their morning coffee and cereal at the dining room table, sharing the papers, then went their separate ways for the morning, occasionally including exercise. They had their own schedules for lunch and afternoon naps or errands. They regrouped again at dinner time. Ginny cooked for the four of them Monday, Tuesday, Thursday and Friday. Wednesday, Saturday, and Sunday, Paul and Joan either cooked or brought food in, or they went out.

"Look at this," Joan held up an article at breakfast that she had printed off her email the day before.

"Big Grandmas and Grandpas," Ginny read. "What is that?"

"I got it from my retired nurses association. They're looking for nurses willing to be Big Grandmas or Grandpas. They match you up with a family with a medically fragile child at home, and you give respite care."

"That's a good idea."

"But there's more. You do it when the real grandparents are there, so you're training them and making them comfortable with the procedures, so they're not afraid to take care of their grandchild."

"Is that a problem?" Frank thought of how easily Ginny had taken care of the grandkids when they were spending a sick day on the living room couch.

"It can be frightening for grandparents to learn medical procedures...feeding tubes, insulin shots, inhalers, oxygen. Anything they've never done before. They're so afraid of making a mistake and hurting their grandchild. They're nervous and worried about it, so it's harder for them to learn from their kids. These families are already traumatized. The grandparents don't want to get in the way and certainly don't want to make things worse. But when they can watch a peer do it, and learn in a more relaxed setting when they're not the ones in charge, apparently it goes better."

"I can see how that would be helpful," Ginny considered, thankful as always that her four children, while having their share of hospital visits, had never had anything major. "But BIG Grandmas? What kind of name is that?"

"Like Big Brothers and Sisters, I think. You could hardly call them Old Grandmas."

"I suppose. Are you going to volunteer?"

"Maybe. It could be fun, don't you think?"

Despite Joan's enthusiasm, the response around the table was lukewarm at best.

A week later, Joan arrived home from her all-day Big Grandmas and Grandpas orientation session and plopped a thick binder on the dining room table where the others were seated. "Really great news!" she exclaimed happily.

"How was it?" Ginny inquired, observing the flushed cheeks and excitement emanating from her friend.

"Wonderful. And, here's the best part...we can all be involved!"

"Hmm?" Frank's attention switched from the bite of bar-b-qued salmon he was moving to his mouth in delicious anticipation to Joan's expectant face. He was hungry tonight, and he hoped to get on with dinner with the least interruption possible.

"It's so smart, these people really have it together." Joan was beaming. "After the first several months of the program, they recognized that these young families, who are facing either an acute illness or a chronic one, have all been on emergency mode for months. They're barely able to work and care for their children, so all sorts of other things are falling by the wayside. The Big Grandmas would arrive and want to do everything…laundry, shopping, cleaning, and taking care of the children. It was too much. So they've allowed each Grandma to register a support team, people she can call on to help with the non-medical tasks. It's a great idea. And takes the pressure off the real grandparents, too, as they are feeling just as overwhelmed as the parents."

"Sounds good," Paul said, although his tone indicated the full consequences of the "great news" might not have sunk in quite yet.

"So, I brought home the forms. I need you to fill them out so you can pass the background check, and then I can call on you whenever I need you. Isn't that terrific?" Joan had expected a little more enthusiasm from her husband and friends, and tried not to feel hurt in its absence; but then she considered that they were all still a little low energy after the life-changing merging of households. "Well, you'll see," she encouraged them. "It's going to be great."

Three weeks later, the freckled face of a four-year-old boy popped into the window as Joan and Ginny approached a modest home with an overgrown yard and one sadly hanging gutter. "They're here!" he yelled as the door was pulled open.

A young mother shushed her son and welcomed them in.

"I'm Noel," she said. "I just put the baby back down for his nap, I'm hoping he'll stay asleep. That would give you a little jump on the day."

Joan and Ginny entered the hallway of what appeared to be a basic three bedroom rambler. It was evident the home was in crisis mode: toys and laundry everywhere, and a view into the kitchen showed dishes stacked up and counter-tops overflowing.

80

"This is my mom, Ruby," Noel introduced the diminutive grandmother, probably at least ten years younger than Ginny and Joan.

"Thank you so much for coming." Ruby held the two-year-old patient, a pale little girl, devoid of hair and with a nasogastric feeding tube taped to her cheek, who shyly turned her head away from them. "And this is Jessie, and that's JT who let you in."

Ginny and Joan dropped their things on the end of the living room couch, and Ginny began making friends with JT as Joan received instructions from Noel. In a few minutes, the children's father appeared from down the hall, dark circles beneath his eyes.

"Here are all the phone numbers," Noel indicated the sheet by the phone to Joan. "Mom knows them by heart, anyway, but just in case."

"What will you do today? Have something fun planned?" Joan asked the visibly tired parents.

"Well," Noel dropped her voice. "We're going to do a couple errands. I desperately need some new pants and tops. And then," she shot a look at her husband, "we thought we'd check into the Best Western hotel and sleep for a few hours. So really, we can come back at any time. Eight to eight seems like a long day for the first time, don't you think? Even with my mom here?"

"Let's see how it goes," Joan reassured her. "I've heard sometimes kids are super good on the first visit. How about if we try to at least get through lunch and naps?"

"Ready?" Noel's husband stood at the door, a small day bag in his hand.

"I haven't been away from the baby for this long, ever," Noel said. "I'm taking the breast pump."

"We'll be fine, honey, don't worry," Ruby reassured her daughter. "You're only going to be minutes away. I promise we'll call if we need you."

Hugs and kisses all around followed, and then off the parents went.

Ruby closed the door with a sigh and glanced at her new friends. She set Jessie down at her feet, and the tiny girl hugged her legs. "Where would you like to start?"

"You choose," Joan said compassionately. "I'm sure you have a routine for what needs done most."

"It's so hard. I live an hour away and I work, so I can only come on the weekends. Then it's starting all over again with laundry and the kitchen. And mostly, just being with Jessie while she's on the pump." Ruby glanced at the kitchen clock. "We've probably got an hour before the baby wakes up. He's mostly going to want to be held if his mom isn't here. Jessie just finished a feed, so she's good until 11 o'clock. If you'll watch the kids, I'll start on the kitchen, see how far I can get."

"JT and I can play in the living room," Ginny said cheerfully. "Maybe we can fold some of that laundry while we do other things."

"Would you like to read some books?" Joan asked Jessie, who nodded and led the way to the stack of books on the other end of the couch.

Ginny heard running water and the clatter of plates in the kitchen as she made a space among the toys and settled on the hardwood floor. "So, JT, what would you like to do?"

"Let's play trains."

"Okay. I think first we better put some things away to make space for the track."

"I don't want to." He turned his back and struggled to pull out a heavy bin filled with wooden track and train cars.

"Ok, but we can only make the tiniest circle if we don't clean up a bit. But if we cleared the floor, I bet we could make the biggest layout ever. I see you have a lot of track. A *whole* lot of track." Ginny had already observed with some anxiety the same trestle bridge that sent her to the hospital ER, and was considering sliding that piece out of sight under the couch.

"Okay. I want to make a big layout."

"You'll have to tell me where things go. Let's make a game of it. Let's put all the puzzles together and see how many there are."

"Okay."

"What time is it?" Ginny called to Ruby in the kitchen after putting together puzzles for what seemed like hours.

"8:30."

"Oh." Ginny had felt sure it must be much later.

The puzzles got picked up, then the stuffed animals found their way to their cubby, then the Duplo blocks went into their bin.

"What time is it now?" Ginny called again.

"8:45."

"Oh." Ginny hoped the time was going as slowly for the young couple as it was moving for her. Joan seemed to be having a delightful time reading books to Jessie, comfortably seated on the couch, while she was crawling all over the hardwood floor corralling toys.

In another twenty minutes there was cry from the back bedroom, and Ruby soon emerged with a red-cheeked nine-month old with tears streaming. He turned his head at seeing Ginny, and it took his grandmother providing his sippy cup to stem the flow of tears.

"Will he let me hold him, do you think?" Ginny asked from her seat on the floor, now partially surrounded with a Brio layout.

"He likes watching JT, so I think so. I'll bring you a biscuit. He likes those. If I could just have fifteen more minutes, I think I can get the kitchen finished. I only have to do the floor."

"Okay."

The baby eyed her warily but sat on her lap and watched his brother discuss the train set and where each piece should go. Ginny happily advised from her spot, stretching her legs, glad to give her knees a rest after crawling around to establish the first train loop. The baby lasted on her lap for about ten minutes, then wanted down to crawl. Ruby stuck her head around the corner, and realizing the train layout was in imminent peril, brought a tub of baby toys and plunked them down. Happily distracted, the baby began pulling toys out, finally settling on a soft giraffe chew toy.

Joan and Jessie switched to playing with the kitchen set, and JT joined them, playing sweetly with his sister. Ginny kept their little brother entertained by stacking blocks for him to knock over. At eleven, Joan took Jessie to the kitchen and called Ruby, who had headed to the master bedroom to tidy up, to watch her start Jessie's feeding tube pump.

"What's that noise?" Joan asked Ruby, trying to place the sound of running water.

"Oh, that's the back toilet. JT must not have jiggled the handle when he went. It's always running. They haven't had time to get it fixed."

"Well, that's easily taken care of." Joan pulled out her phone and called Frank, instructing him to round up Paul and head over. And to stop somewhere and bring lunch. "Will you eat a turkey sandwich?" she asked Ruby.

"Of course, sounds good."

"All right, then. Reinforcements are on the way. Now, let's get this feed started."

Ruby watched as Joan went through the steps to get the formula primed into the pump and everything ready to go.

"I know it probably seems complicated at first, but it's not too difficult. These new pumps make it pretty easy once you get used to their prompts."

"I've watched Noel do it a million times, but I don't feel comfortable doing it myself. I'm afraid I'll mess it up. Sometimes the pump jams, or it won't run. I don't want to be the one it breaks on."

"Take it step by step." Joan took the stethoscope from the counter top and then sent a small pop of air through the feeding tube with an empty syringe as she listened to Jessie's belly. "Okay, heard it loud and clear."

"That's the part I'm afraid of," Ruby confided. "What if I can't hear the noise?"

"Have you ever tried?"

Ruby shook her head no.

"It's really very clear. Next time, you listen."

"But what if I can't hear it?"

"Then you just do it again. It's so unlikely that the tube has pulled out of the stomach, it's a precaution, that all. But really, the pop of air is quite clear. Once you know what to listen for, you'll recognize it."

"Okay. I'll try it the next time, if you're right here with me."

Joan connected the line carrying the formula into the end of Jessie's nasogastric tube and double checked the settings. She hit "Run" and the pump came to life, sending the formula through the tube into Jessie's stomach.

"Now what does Jessie do while she's on the pump?"

Ruby zipped up the flaps of the small backpack that held the little pump. "She can do anything, but you pretty much have to stay with her. She's too little to carry the backpack on her back, so we carry it around for her. And if the pump falls over it quits running sometimes and you have to start over. So I usually just read books to her if I'm here. Or we do puzzles or color at the table. It takes about 25 minutes to run."

Soon JT was at the front door again, helping to greet Frank and Paul who arrived carrying food bags.

"Plumber!" Frank called cheerfully as he came through the door.

"Really?" asked the four-year-old, who tagged along as Frank was directed to the back bathroom.

Five minutes later they were back out, with Frank heading to the hardware. "It really needs a new fill valve. I'll be back soon."

"What can I do to help?" Paul asked no one in particular.

"Could you come hold this baby?" Ginny called from the living room. "I need to get up off the floor."

Paul gently took the little boy, covered with teething drool and pieces of mushed hard biscuit, and settled into a nearby chair, carefully keeping his charge pointed toward the others so he wouldn't notice the change. Ginny painfully rose and extricated herself from the Brio set.

"What time is it, anyway?" she asked Paul.

"Eleven forty-five."

"Oh, man," she stretched her aching joints. "It's going to be a long day."

When the young parents arrived home two hours early because Noel was unable to stay away from her children any longer, the young mother burst into tears when she walked through the front door. Even from that partial vantage point, she could see the kitchen was clean, the floors had been swept, and the pile of laundry on the couch had been folded and put away. JT was playing in a tidy living room with a gentleman she didn't know, soup simmered on the stove, and her mom was disconnecting Jessie from the pump.

"Welcome home," Joan greeted her gently. "I hope you had a good day."

"We fell asleep at one and didn't wake up till five," her husband said, giving Jessie a big hug. "Missed you, baby girl," he whispered in her ear.

"I only woke up because my breasts were so full I had to pump again," Noel said, snuggling her baby, who, apparently sensing the milk supply was home, tried to burrow through her shirt. "Thank you so much. And all this housework you did. I never expected that."

"It took five of us to get this far," Ginny spoke up. "We all remember what it's like with a baby in the house, and that was without an ill toddler!"

In bed that evening, completely drained, one last thought flitted through Ginny's brain. When she closed her eyes, all she could see was a mountain of toys and train track.

"Next time…" she mumbled to Frank.

"…we'll take Alex to play with JT."

"Right."

They were silent for a few minutes before Frank spoke again. "You know, I'd like to go back and fix that gutter before the wood rots on that side."

Ginny smiled but was asleep before Frank could turn off the light.

Chapter Eighteen

Little Francie and Mara had fallen asleep quickly in the guest room twin beds, exhausted from their fun day with their grandmother and grandfather. After checking to be sure the pillow fighting had stopped, Ginny joined Frank, Paul, and Joan at the dining room table for coffee and the rest of a deep-dish apple pie topped with French vanilla ice cream.

"I know I'm not the first to think this, but they look like such angels when they're sleeping." Ginny slid into her chair in exhaustion. "You'd never guess they'd broken a window, dented the car, and run over my newly planted primroses."

"Is it always like this?" Joan inquired. Lindsay and Mo's children (seven-year-old Alex and his older sisters) were active, but paled in comparison to their cousins, the two little tornadoes with whom she'd spent the afternoon.

"The girls are energetic, but we don't usually have breakage," Frank said. "It was a rougher day than usual, I'm not sure why."

Paul smiled thinking of the girls playing baseball on the cool spring afternoon with a big red bat. "I think it's because Mara has learned how to connect with the ball. That girl can swing! Who knew a hard plastic ball could dent a Subaru?"

"I guess we should have quit playing after she broke the garage window," Frank said. "I still can't figure out how she got that angle on the ball from where we had home plate."

"Going back to angels," Ginny served herself the last piece of pie and scooped the softened ice cream onto it. "I've been wishing Robert and Jill would get them baptized. I don't know why they don't go to church, they were both brought up in it. I know lots of young people stop going for a while, but usually once they have kids they wander back to the fold. I don't know what's happened."

"Why don't you ask them?" Paul said.

"You have to be careful what you say when it's your daughter-in-law, not your daughter, don't you think?" Ginny replied.

"I don't know," Joan smiled. "I've got boys. Our daughter-in-law is your daughter, and you seem to cover anything I'm thinking before I have to broach the subject!"

"We've got it easy with Lindsay and Mo, that's for sure," Ginny agreed. "But, I was thinking. Paul, you're still ordained, right, even though you turned to teaching and haven't had your own church for a long time? You can still do the sacraments?"

"Yes, although I'm not sure I like where this is going."

"Couldn't you go up and baptize them in their sleep? No one would even need to know but us four."

"Baptism isn't magic, Ginny, you know that. It's promises made to the community, *in* the community. Usually by the parents or guardians."

"I don't see why grandparents can't make the promises."

Paul studied his good friend, trying to decide which way to take the conversation. "Well, beyond teaching the kids some of the basics like the Lord's Prayer and Ten Commandments, one of the promises is to bring the children to church. You can't drag Mara and Francie to church over their parents' objection."

"*Drag?* You make it sound so negative, and you're even a minister."

"What's bringing this up?" Paul asked curiously.

Ginny put her fork down and regarded her friend honestly. "We had a baptism at church last week, and it reminded me that Mara and Francie are the only grandkids who aren't baptized. I haven't been able to do anything about it before this, but *now* I've got a minister living in the house."

"I admire your initiative, but your time would be better spent broaching the subject with Robert and Jill. I repeat, baptism isn't some magic safety potion." Paul paused thoughtfully for a moment before finishing. "Although, considering the combined energy level of the lively little angels you've got asleep upstairs, I sympathize and understand your concern."

"What good's a live-in minister if you can't get a simple sacrament when you need one?" Ginny muttered as she picked up her plate and began to clear the table.

"Ooooh, there's an idea. Sacraments on demand," Joan said. "I'm surprised no one's thought of that and put up an internet service. Retired pastors on-call or something."

"I think we'd be pushing the theological envelope with sacraments for pay. Martin Luther would be rolling in his grave," Paul reminded his wife.

"Oh, fine. I'll figure out another way," Ginny came back into the room. "Easter's coming up. Maybe we can get them to church with the bribe of new Easter dresses. Mara and Francie are rough and tumble, but they still have soft spot for princess dresses. Thank you, Walt Disney."

"Why don't you pray about it?" Paul turned the conversation serious again. "Can't hurt, might help."

Frank woke up after midnight and realized Ginny wasn't in bed beside him. Seeing a shadow cast from the hall's nightlight, he got up to investigate. Ginny was just exiting the little girls' room, a small bowl and a cloth in her hand.

"What are you doing?" he whispered.

"Sh."

"Don't shush me. What on earth are you doing?"

"I thought they seemed feverish. A cool cloth."

"For heaven's sake, I thought Paul talked some sense into you at dinner. What happened to praying about it?"

"I did pray. I prayed I wouldn't get caught."

"You're impossible. You know that, don't you?"

Ginny shrugged and indicated the bowl of water in her hands. "Can't hurt, might help."

Chapter Nineteen

Lindsay carried plates to the kitchen while her parents, in-laws and siblings remained on the patio, enjoying the afternoon sun and watching the youngest children play in the backyard. It had been an enjoyable picnic after a morning of shopping with her older girls while the four grandparents looked after Alex. Lindsay continued to be amazed at the smooth transition both sets of parents had made to the new living arrangement. She kept waiting for disaster to strike, but so far, they had all seemed congenial and happy.

Alex suddenly popped up beside her at the sink. "Can I go to Home Depot with Papa?"

"When do you think he's going?" Lindsay asked, as there had been no mention of a trip to her father's favorite store during the meal.

"I don't know." Alex took a chocolate chip cookie from the plate on the counter. "They need buckets for something."

"Buckets?"

"Yeah, they were making a list of buckets to get."

A quizzical frown crossed Lindsay's face, not that buying a wide variety of buckets would be that unusual for her dad.

"I'll show you," Alex continued. "I know where they put the shopping list."

"I don't want you snooping through their house. That's impolite."

"No, it's right here. Noni was cleaning up the kitchen this morning and said, 'I'm putting the bucket list under the dish towels where no one will ever see it.'"

Now Alex had her full attention. "Noni called it a *bucket list?*"

"Yeah."

Lindsay grabbed Mo from the hall and dragged him to the kitchen. Alex pulled open the third drawer down beside the stove, rooted under the neatly folded dish towels, and pulled out a page of lined notebook paper. Lindsay examined it thoughtfully, showing the neat list in his mother's printing to Mo. "A bucket list," she mused. "Look, honey, our parents are on the move."

The next weekend, Lindsay arrived in time to see her father-in-law drive up in a forty-foot RV, bringing home a possible rental for the others' inspection.

Chapter Twenty

"Mom?" Ginny recognized an uncharacteristic panic in her daughter's voice. The last time she'd heard that tone was when Lindsay announced her pregnancy with Alex, which, at the time, had been unplanned, unexpected, and seemingly world-ending. Instead, the arrival of the dear little boy had been nothing but delight.

"Mom, are you there?"

"Yes, honey, I'm sorry. What's up?"

"Alex's school called. They're closing the entire school. Thirty percent of the sixth graders have a virus…noro or rotor or something like that. They're closing the school for the week!"

"I'm sorry, honey. Do you need us to go get Alex?"

"Yes, but it's more than that. I'm trying to get ten employees reassigned before layoff notices go out, and Mo has a new product launch this week. None of my backup sitters can take Alex because they have kids, and no one wants to be anywhere near a kid from his school."

Ginny glanced around her kitchen, with the neat piles of food supplies she and Joan had organized for their week-long trip. Frank and Paul were inspecting the motor home at this very moment, checking and rechecking fluid levels and whatever else people do when they look under a hood and chassis.

"I know you're supposed to leave on your trip tomorrow…."

"Yes, Dad and Paul are working on the motor home right now. Of course I can go get Alex and bring him here for the rest of today. But—"

"I was thinking," Lindsay interrupted with her most convincing and hopeful voice in full play, "could Alex go with you? It would be educational. He loves you all so much, you know he's no trouble at all compared Mara and Francie. You'd barely know he was along."

"I wouldn't go that far, dear," Ginny sighed. "Let me talk to Paul and Joan. They're not as used to the full-time grandparent thing as we are. And this is our maiden voyage in the motor home. I don't even know how well the four of us will do in such close quarters."

"You and Dad get lots of extra grandparent points for being fully available, I know. And we ever so appreciate that you are not travelers and wanderers like Paul and Joan, and have bailed us out so many times before. But this one is bad, Mom. They're cutting back at work, if I take a week off right now...."

"Stop the guilt trip already. I'll go pick up Alex then I'll talk to the others and call you back."

And so the next morning, bright and early, with Frank at the wheel, Paul riding shotgun, and Joan and Ginny settling the cheerful Alex in his seat in happy expectation, his little suitcase stowed under the eating bench, his backpack filled with books, games, and toys tucked beside him, and his pillow and sleeping bag close at hand, the adventurers set off for the sixty minute drive to the campgrounds north of Seattle. It seemed a good trial run: easy rig hookups, a lake with canoe and small boat rentals, a tennis court and plenty of space.

Ginny was admiring the smooth ride, when Alex interrupted her thoughts.

"Noni, I have to go to the bathroom."

"Darling, didn't you go at home before we left? We've only been on the freeway for two minutes."

"I did but I have to go again."

"All right. We showed you how to use the travel toilet...go ahead."

"I can't go while the motor home is moving."

"Oh, honey, of course you can," Joan addressed him gently. "That's the whole idea of a motor home, you can move around a little while you travel."

"No," Alex shook his head vehemently. "Mom said not to take off my seat belt while the motor home is moving"

"Oh, for heaven's sake," Frank grumbled from behind the wheel.

"That sounds like Lindsay," Ginny admitted. "But look, sweetie, like on your school bus in the morning, you don't have seat belts on there, do you? If you have to get up and move to another seat, that's okay, right?"

"Only if Mrs. Collins says you can because someone's bothering you. I really have to go, Papa," Alex addressed the driver somewhat urgently.

"I'll go with you," Paul popped off his seatbelt and offered his hand to his grandson, ever so pleased this was shaping up to be a Lindsay incident and not a Mo one. "Come on."

"No, Mom made me promise I'd keep my seat belt on while we were moving."

"Frank…" Ginny used her best "we have to" voice. "Can you find a place to pull over?"

"Not really. We're right in the middle of Lynnwood. Give me a couple minutes, I can take the mall exit. Can you wait five minutes, buddy?"

"I guess so," Alex said morosely.

"Well," Joan said brightly. "Off to a great start. At this rate we'll make the campgrounds by midnight."

Ginny swallowed the choice words that were pushing their way to her lips. The couples had never fought, but if they did, it would be over the parenting practices of their adult children. Lindsay had her faults, but it wasn't like Mo was perfect. He was useless in any kind of medical crisis and fainted at the sight of blood. ("It's a vagal reflex, he

96

can't help it," Joan had explained early on, as they picked Mo up off the floor at the first grandchild's birth.) Oh, well, she wouldn't let these negative thoughts ruin the trip.

They completed the drive to the county campground with two more stops for Alex. Ginny was beginning to get an uneasy feeling about his sudden intestinal distress, but her grandson seemed cheery otherwise, and after getting settled in their campsite, they had a fun afternoon exploring the lake.

The dinner of hot dogs and baked beans, followed by S'mores around a small campfire, did not sit well, however, and ten minutes after he was settled in his sleeping bag, Alex called out for help and erupted.

Between Joan and Ginny, they managed to make him comfortable. Paul made several trips to the soda machines for ginger ale to ease Alex's upset stomach, while Ginny wished she had thought to throw in her old standby, a hot water bottle.

On the next day, they took turns staying with Alex, who was slowly on the mend, and wandering around the campgrounds. Ginny was looking for birds and Joan enjoyed people watching along the lake.

That evening, Frank was the first to feel ill; Ginny got it the next morning, and finally Paul succumbed. From her years of nursing, Joan seemed to have built up resistance to this particular virus, and she managed to stay on her feet tending the others and occupying Alex. This bug was the vicious kind that led to vomiting with such intensity even the adults could not make it to the bathroom, and if they had, it would have been occupied anyway as everyone was having the runs, also. Joan had distributed the few pots and bowls they had to keep by their beds, but they were out of sheets, towels, toilet paper and, more importantly, any kind of fluid that would re-hydrate the crew.

On the fourth morning, Joan went to the back bedroom and observed Frank, prostrate on his side with a towel propped beneath his head.

97

"Frank," she whispered, so as not to disturb Ginny, who had her head at the opposite end of the bed, similarly propped with a towel and wrapped in blankets.

"Frank," she whispered more forcefully.

"Yeah," Frank opened one eye and wondered why there were two of Joan standing before him.

"Frank, we have to get you all home. This is getting serious. I have no more fluids for you, and it could be another twelve hours before you're over it. Is there any way you can drive?"

"I don't think so, Joan. I'm seeing two of you right now."

"Okay. Well, then I think I have to drive this thing. Can't be that much harder than a van, right? It's automatic, it just goes, right? There's no wind, roads are dry...I'll just point it south."

"I don't know, Joan. It's forty feet. But I guess if you go slow, and give yourself plenty of space to pull out on the freeway. All you have to do is unhook the water and electricity. I'll take care of the sewage at home. Get the camp manager to help you."

"Okay, you rest. It'll be fine. Alex will help." Joan felt fairly confident; surely unplugging this big rig could not be much more difficult than detaching patients from their IVs and catheters.

After being sure her husband and friends were snuggly tucked in, Joan and her assistant Alex secured the help of the campground manager to get the rig ready to roll. Sitting in the captain's chair, Joan observed the cockpit-like dashboard, checking for the lights, blinkers, wipers, and parking brake release.

"Do you want to ride shotgun and help me?" she asked Alex, who beamed at the request.

First she took three circles around the campground road to get the feel of the steering, with the manager standing in their spot giving her a "good to go" thumbs up on her third pass. She practiced with the brakes, as her first attempt caused groans from her prone, vulnerable passengers and the seat belt jerked on Alex. "Pretty touchy," she mused to herself.

Luckily, it was only a few miles of well-paved road to Interstate 5. As it was mid-morning, traffic was moderate and she eased her forty-foot ship onto the far right lane, slowly increased her speed to 55, and tried to hold the steering wheel steady. Checking her mirrors, she watched fast traffic speed up and overtake her. The large trucks were a little frightening as they seemed to both suck her sideways and then blow her the opposite way as they went by. She concentrated on the timing to be more prepared when she saw a big truck coming up. Her hands slowly quit sweating, and she and Alex sang a few songs to ease the tension. She'd been driving for about forty minutes when she saw flashing lights in the mirror. Expecting the patrol car to pass her, she slowed a bit more, but instead he fell in behind her at her speed.

"Paul!" she called to her husband, who was lying motionless above her in the loft bed. "I've got the State Patrol with lights on behind me. What should I do?"

"Are you sure he's for you?"

"He's been there a couple minutes now. I don't know what to do. I can't stop here."

"Put on your blinker and slow down. Look for an exit or any wide place where you could pull over."

"I don't want to get off the freeway. What if I can't get turned around? And the shoulder is all rough and slanted. Wait, there's a little bridge up ahead, it's wide before it."

"No!" Frank yelled from the back. "Not at an overpass!"

"Keep going," Paul said. "He'll know you're trying to stop."

"Look, Grandma, up there." Alex pointed ahead. "It's pretty wide where those cars are coming on. After the bridge."

Joan saw the particularly wide, paved area ahead on the right side. She slowed even further, carefully negotiated through the two cars who were making a freeway entrance, and drifted to a stop at the side of the road.

The State Patrol unit pulled in behind her at a protective angle, and she watched as the officer approached her window. It took a minute but she finally slid the pane open and started before the officer could even begin.

"I'm so sorry, Officer, I couldn't pull over sooner. I needed to find a safe place."

"Yes, ma'am. Do you mind opening your front door there so I can come around on the other side?" He was peering up at her from his disadvantaged lower station.

"Of course, please, yes, get out of the traffic." With Alex pointing out the correct lever, she opened the front door.

"May I see your license and registration?" the officer asked politely.

"I'll have to get it, my purse is in the back. This is a rental, I'm not quite sure where the registration is. Was there a problem, officer?"

"We had several calls about a motor home impeding traffic and drifting out of their lane."

"Oh." Joan's feelings were hurt, as she thought she'd been driving quite well. Then the realization struck her. "Oh, dear, I hope you don't think I'm intoxicated. It's not that. I've never driven this rig before. The others are all sick with a norovirus. We—" she motioned to Alex—"had to pack up by ourselves this morning and I'm trying to get us home. The others need fluids, we're completely out of towels and toilet paper, and I couldn't really drive this thing to the neighborhood grocery. I'd never be able to park it and I'm afraid of getting stuck and—"

"Ma'am, would you step out of the vehicle, please?"

"Of course. Alex, grab my purse. It's on the counter by the stove."

"It's all right, son, just sit where you are."

Alex's face was full of excitement but a little concern. "Grandma?"

"Just sit here, honey, it's okay. Do what the officer says. He's trying to be sure everything is all right."

Joan grabbed her purse and stepped out into the bright sunlight as the officer keenly observed her.

"Who all is in the rig with you?"

Feeling more confident now that the first command hadn't been a sobriety field test, Joan replied, "It's my husband, Paul. He's in the overhead sleeper. Our friends, actually our son's in-laws, are in the back bedroom. Ginny and Frank. They all came down with this virus the day before yesterday. Alex had it three days ago. He's our grandson. All of ours grandson. His school got closed because so many kids were sick, and our son and daughter-in-law asked if we'd take him with us this week, as they were desperate. I wasn't really worried if he got sick. I'm a nurse. But I hadn't counted on the others becoming ill." Joan took a breath while carefully observing the young officer, to be sure he was fully following. "It's not that unusual of a virus, but for kids and older folks like us, dehydration can be a problem. So I really need to get these people home this morning where I can take care of them." Joan could still not discern whether she was making the proper impression. Did the officer think she was transporting drugs or something? Was talking so much helping or hurting?

"Would you mind if I stepped into the motor home?"

"Not at all." Joan waited at the bottom of the steps. "You might hold your breath," she called after him. "It's pretty contagious. There have been fluid particles flying every direction for the last 48 hours." Joan fished her driver's license out of her purse as she spoke, and noted the officer made a quick retreat at the mention of flying fluids. She held out her license as he returned to fresh air. The smell inside the motor home was more pronounced than she had realized.

101

"Okay, ma'am. Obviously, the concern was an impaired driver, which is not the case. I can see you feel you're in emergency mode here."

"I'm sorry if I was driving slowly. I was trying to go 55. The passing trucks were a challenge. But I *was* staying in my lane. Most of the time."

"How far are you from home?"

"We just have to get to Ballinger...Exit 177. So...another 30 minutes?"

"Once there, do you have a pretty clear shot to your houses?"

"Oh, yes. Only about three stop lights and two turns."

"All right, you can return to your seat. I'll be back in a moment."

He still had her license, and Alex handed the rental papers, which Frank had informed him where to find, out the door. After five minutes the officer returned and handed the papers and license back to Joan.

"Okay, Mrs. Rogers. Here's what we're going to do. First, another unit is a few minutes away. He's going to lead you back on the freeway. Then I'll follow you to your exit. You're really not a danger to anyone in front of you...since there's no one in front of you. But I'll keep folks off your tail, and the trucks will keep to the speed limit when they see me, and that will help with the wind effect when they pass you."

"Oh, thank you so much. I was just nervous at first, that's all. I think my driving had really improved by the time you caught up to us."

"Yes. Well. I'm assuming you don't need immediate medical help right here?"

"Oh, no, another 12 hours without fluids and we'd be in trouble, but I think we'll be fine once I can roll everyone into their own beds. We all live together, actually. It will be quite convenient."

"You all....oh, never mind. Here's our escort. He's going to go in front," the officer waved the other patrol car to stop adjacent to

102

them and roll down his window. "When she gives you the signal she's ready," he nodded back to Joan, who shook her head that she understood, "go ahead and lead her out."

Joan started up the rig.

Paul looked out the forward facing window of his bunk to see the front patrol unit leading them, but he was too sick to enjoy the excitement. Alex, however, was beaming.

Joan had no more trouble steering, and an hour later had rolled her sick crew into their respective beds at home and was serving up Gatorade and popsicles.

Ginny snuggled under the blankets beside her husband, her head still achy and the room spinning slightly.

"Next time…" she mumbled to Frank, whose eyes were tightly closed against the sun peeking through the misaligned curtains, "next time—"

"No kids." Frank finished the sentence for her firmly.

Chapter Twenty-One

"So there they were, sick as dogs, and Joan had no choice but to drive home," Lindsay recounted the saga to Tess after pulling into her driveway.

"It's a miracle she got that thing home. They're not that easy to drive, I don't think."

"I guess once the State Patrol accompanied her, she didn't have as much trouble. Alex thought it was a great time, surrounded by police vehicles. We've probably started a fascination with True Crime. His favorite part was the lights and siren. Meanwhile, the motor home is still sitting in front of their house. Dad isn't out of bed yet."

"What's next on their bucket list, do you know? How funny that you used to complain your mom had no spirit of adventure!"

"She always said raising the four of us was enough adventure for a lifetime. I know she's had her fill for the moment. But the others are raring to go. But how's *your* mom doing this week?" Lindsay had many fond memories of afternoons sitting on the porch at Tess's house, being regaled by Betty's stories of growing up on a farm in eastern Washington as she smoked her way through a pack of cigarettes. Even compared to Mo's more adventurous parents, Betty had been on the wild side her entire life, according to Tess.

"Oh, nothing new. She spent three days last week at the casino. Came home ahead this time. Course that only makes her more anxious to go back up. Her cough is so much worse, but I can't get her to go to the doctor, or use her oxygen. She practically turns blue sometimes.

104

I guess we'll wait till she keels over and lands in the hospital, then maybe she'll listen to someone."

"Do you think the emphysema is progressing? She's still seems so independent."

"Between the emphysema and the heart failure, I feel like *I'm* the mother waiting for the middle-of-the night phone call about my wayward child. Only the child is 75 and should know better than to be out all night. If she would just take care of herself a little, and quit smoking. That alone would help a lot."

"Here comes Mo, I've got to go. I'm hoping he's got dinner on the front seat."

"Okay," Tess was parked at the grocery store waiting to find some dinner for her own kids. "Talk to you tomorrow. Glad your folks got home safe. Alex is going to have quite a tale to tell."

"Yeah. I think we might have used up our last emergency babysitting card on this one. I'll need to think of something pretty wonderful to do to get back in their good graces. I really didn't think Alex was going to get sick."

"Yeah, right," Tess sighed, having been on the wrong end of emergency kid coverage that ended up bringing down her whole household more than once, "that's what they all say."

Chapter Twenty-Two

Paul was sitting at the table after dinner, paging through his AAA British Columbia tour guide book.

"Let's go to Horseshoe Bay," he announced to no one in particular.

"Where is that?" Ginny asked from the other side of the table where she was working on the morning's crossword puzzle.

"Just a little north of Vancouver. It would be an easy drive, less than three hours. And it's beautiful there. There's a little campground right on the water. It'd be perfect." The April weather was inconsistent but warming up, and Paul was itching to get going somewhere.

"We were there in the summer of 1975," Joan said. "I don't know why we haven't been back. It's one of the most magnificent places on earth. The sky was blue, then these snow-capped mountains come right down to the water. Gorgeous." She closed the book she had been reading in her living room chair. "That's a perfect choice, Paul."

"What would you all think about taking a smaller rig this time? Then if we want to go into Vancouver, it would be easier to park. The weather should be good, maybe just cool. We'll be outside most of the time, just need a place to sleep." Paul surveyed his companions' faces to determine their willingness to get back in a motor home.

"Fine with me," said Frank. "I'm game."

"One small problem. I don't have a passport," Ginny said.

Joan looked at her with surprise. "You mean it's expired?"

"No," Ginny said a bit defensively. "I don't have one."

"You've never traveled outside the country?" Paul tried to keep the incredulousness from his voice. He had known Ginny for so many years, yet it had never registered that her travel had been in-country only.

"No," Ginny was defiant now. "You know I'm a farmer not a traveler. There wasn't ever a need to go far off. Frank traveled for work, sometimes, but I stayed home with the kids."

"Then you are overdue for a real treat," Paul said heartily. "First order of business tomorrow, we'll work on your passport. It's easy, there's an office in north Seattle with good hours. I hate to ask this, but do you have your birth certificate?"

"Of course. In the 'important' folder in the file drawer."

Ginny lay awake in bed that night, pondering another trip. She had no little children that needed care to use as an excuse this time. And Vancouver was practically next door. Not much farther than Portland, just north instead of south. And Horseshoe Bay sounded lovely. She'd give it her best try, for Frank's sake.

Three weeks later, Ginny had her expedited passport in hand. She had fussed a bit over getting a good picture for it, but finally gave in to Joan's advice of a plain white blouse. Ginny held her passport and turned the blank pages. Joan and Paul's were filled with stamps, each page a memory of an adventure together. Hers, on the other hand, looked rather pathetic, empty page after empty page.

Starting later than expected after lunch, the entry into Canada went smoothly. The smaller rig wasn't nearly as comfortable as the big motor home had been, but the pull-out bench beds would be bearable for a few nights. Ginny enjoyed seeing the Peace Arch at the border crossing, and did get a little thrill being on British Columbia soil.

The unpredicted rain started falling twenty minutes after crossing the border, as they made their way into Vancouver. Frank drove, with

Paul acting as navigator and tour guide, calling out sights which Ginny had difficulty seeing through the downpour hitting against the glass.

"Maybe we'll stop on our way home," Paul said as they passed various spots he remembered from other trips. "You'll love Stanley Park."

Making their way down to the campgrounds on the far side of Vancouver, Ginny felt as if she were being swallowed into an abyss. The temperature had cooled considerably and she couldn't really see out the windows.

"I don't know where this rain is coming from," Frank muttered as he drove cautiously. "We've got to get that radar approved off Washington's coast so we know better what's coming. This is ridiculous."

"It's not far now," Paul said, double checking his map.

"I'm sorry you can't see the mountain tops," Joan sighed as she observed the heavy, low hanging clouds. "They should be covered with snow. The contrast to the blue sky and blue water was breathtaking."

A dark funk enveloped Ginny. She pulled on her extra jacket to keep out the chill and reminded herself again to be a good sport instead of wishing she were home pulling weeds.

They found the campgrounds and their reserved spot. Hooked up their electricity, water and waste lines in the rain. Joan ran back to the check-in booth and brought back a brochure of things to do.

"I guess we'll settle in for the day, if that's okay," Frank said. "I'd rather not drive back up that hill again at the moment."

"No problem. I saw a little fish and chips stand. We could get dinner there."

The foursome donned their standard Seattle just-in-case rain jackets and dashed for the fish shack. Its interior was a bit dark and cold, and the outside seating was being pummeled by rain, so they returned to the rig to eat.

"Well, this is cozy," Ginny observed between bites. At least the fish was truly delicious, even if only lukewarm by the time it made it to her mouth.

"I'm sure tomorrow will dawn bright and beautiful," Frank said. "The weather report really wasn't calling for rain. I checked several times."

"Oh, you know what it's like predicting weather in the Pacific Northwest," Ginny argued. "Wait five minutes and something else will be happening."

Bundled in warm clothes, the four played a few hands of bridge after dinner, then pulled out their beds and hunkered down to read. The rain tapped steadily on the roof as they drifted off to sleep one by one. Ginny, the last to turn off her light, was not getting the feeling that the morning was going to dawn bright and clear.

And it didn't. After continuous showers in the morning, in which the intrepid explorers tromped along the water's edge getting soaked, they stopped at a small convenience store. Frank inquired about the weather from the shopkeeper. Informed that the forecast had changed from light rain to a "steady downpour" for the next twenty-four hours, the group reconvened for lunch in the rig, giving themselves a chance to dry out.

"I'm sorry," Paul said. "It's so beautiful. It's right there, through the fog, I can't tell you how close we are to magnificence."

Hidden splendor or not, no one was in the mood to linger any longer, or to try to find their way around Vancouver in the rig and their wet shoes.

By dinner time, they were across the border, past the Peace Arch, through the evening commuter traffic, and parked in front of their own home, where it was not raining. Joan and Paul drove out to pick up some Thai food, while Ginny unpacked the unused groceries from the rig.

"Well, that was an adventure," Ginny greeted Joan brightly as the good-smelling dinner arrived home. "I think I'll bake some cookies," she added, always happy to be home in her own kitchen. "Maybe some of the kids will be by tomorrow now that they know we're back. The little girls would probably like to play house in the rig, since we have it till Tuesday."

Frank shook his head, mumbling that it was a lot of money for a playhouse for the girls.

"I'm sure it was a beautiful spot," Ginny consoled him. "We'll see it next time. It's like Mount Rainier...you never know when it will be out in all its glory."

"I guess so," Frank said. "And hey, at least you've got a passport now!"

"I certainly do," Ginny said, although fairly certain she'd be putting the small booklet in the important folder where it might sit for quite some time.

"So they weren't even there for twenty-four hours," Lindsay told Tess later that evening. "It was raining so hard, and they were in a smaller rig, they just packed up and came home. Dad said Mom started baking almost the minute she walked in the door. We're heading over there tomorrow."

"I give your mom points for trying. I'm shocked they even got her out of the country."

"Yeah, well, they're zip for two now on travel, after the disaster with Alex. I'm not sure how many more tries Mom will give them before she gives up. I think maybe she really was a farmer in a former life. She'd be perfectly content milking a cow twice a day and collecting eggs in a henhouse."

110

"You know, that's an idea. I bet you could find a place to go that's a working farm. Maybe she'd like that."

"Only if they'd let her in the kitchen. She always just says she's a content person, and wonders why the rest of us aren't. It's an interesting question."

"Well, I wouldn't complain if my mom were a little more content," Tess grumbled. "She's hitting the casino four days a week now. I told her I didn't want her driving I-5 anymore. She's a menace when she starts to cough, she can hardly keep the car in the lane. So now she catches a bus the casino runs from the North End transportation center at Northgate. You've got to hand it to the casinos; they make it pretty easy for you to come and spend money."

"Is she overspending?"

"I have no idea. She's never discussed money with us, only says things are fine. I know Dad made a good living, and I think he had an inheritance from his family, too. He never talked about finances to us kids, and even if he did, I don't know if we would have believed him. He tended to exaggerate a bit depending on how much he'd had to drink. The older I get, the more amazed I am he managed to be so functional in terms of work. High functioning alcoholic, I guess."

"There are more of them than you'd think, supposedly. But your mom sure loved him. I have a lot memories of them together."

"They were very dependent on each other, in a weird kind of way. I wish he were still here to help with mom right now."

Lindsay tried to think of something positive to say. "What do you think about getting your mom interested in an assisted living place? I still have all the literature from my folks' attempt. Do you want it?"

Tess sighed. "I guess. I really should start looking, but it was like moving heaven and earth to get her out of the house into an apartment. I can't imagine what it will take to get her to move again."

Tess was silent a minute, and then asked hopefully, "I don't suppose you found any that allowed smoking, did you?"

Chapter Twenty-Three

Sitting at the breakfast table, Frank perused an article in the newspaper about five Boeing F/A-18 Super Hornets heading to the Royal Australian Air Force, the first of twenty-four. "The only thing I miss from the Air Force is flying a small plane," he said. "I'd love to fly again."

"Let's put it on the bucket list," Joan said excitedly. "We could all four go somewhere."

"Not me," Ginny interrupted. "I'm terra firma."

"Oh, come on. It would be great fun. We could take Kenmore Air somewhere. How about that, Frank?" The single-engine float planes were a far cry from military jets, but that was a small detail to Joan.

"Sure, that would do. And I've never done a water landing. How about you Paul, are you in?"

Paul had been concentrating on his crossword puzzle. "Sure." He was usually game for whatever the others were planning.

"I'll be the designated survivor and stay home to watch," Ginny informed them. "Wave when you go over the house."

"Kenmore Air has an impeccable safety rating," Frank cajoled his intractable wife. "Landing on water, they have so many places to put down around here even if there is an emergency."

Joan got a great idea. "When we tell them you're a pilot, I'll bet they let you sit up front. Maybe even in the co-pilot seat!"

"Well, if they let you in the cockpit," Ginny warned dryly, "don't touch anything."

Three weeks later, the day dawned bright and clear, as promised. Frank had studiously checked the ten-day forecast the entire week before, to be sure of the most auspicious day for their tour with Kenmore Air.

Ginny sent them off with a smile. She had some fun planned for herself, and it would start as soon as she was sure the adventurers were on their way with no returns for forgotten items.

Thirty minutes later, Ginny had carefully made her way onto the low-pitch, upper roof of her home, with a can of temporary, bright orange spray paint in her hand. "This is going to be so good," she said to herself proudly.

She pondered for a few moments, trying to decide which way the letters should face, and finally decided to line up with the usual landing pattern of the float planes that went over their home daily, to and from the small marina airport at the north end of Lake Washington. They had all become accustomed to the overhead buzz of the small pontooned aircraft as they landed and took off each day.

Ginny had finished her careful inspiration when her cell phone buzzed, indicating a text. She ignored it, but her phone went off again. Putting down her spray can, she fished the phone from her pocket, flipping it open. Her children had been unable to convince her to try one of the newer smart phones, so it took a few seconds for her to find the text from her neighbor two doors down and across the street.

"Are you okay?!" the text printed.

"Yes. Why?" Ginny was not a speedy texter.

"There are three police officers creeping up on your house right now."

Ginny walked over the roof peak to the street side in an effort to see better. Her neighbor was standing on the sidewalk in front of her own house, behind a police cruiser. Ginny waved, then texted again.

"Why?"

"They got a report of a woman in distress on a roof."

Oh, for heaven's sake, Ginny thought irritably. "Caroline!!" she yelled, rather than wasting time texting. "Tell them I'm fine."

She watched Caroline cross the street and disappear from sight, then three officers accompanied her and stood on Ginny's front sidewalk. One of them, Officer Dewey, she recognized from various Block Watch meetings.

"Mrs. Noonan? Are you all right?" Officer Dewey called.

"I'm perfectly fine. I'm doing a special project. The roof is low-pitched, I'm perfectly safe."

A fire truck now ambled down the street, lights on but no siren.

"We'll be right up," the middle officer called.

"No...really, no, you don't have to..."

"May we enter your home?" the third officer shouted. "Once we get a distress call, we have to check things out."

"The back door's open. But really, everything's fine."

She watched as the firefighters unloaded their tall ladder and plunked it against the side of the house. She was going to offer some advice, but the first fireman, followed by Officer Dewey, was up the ladder before she could get their attention.

"Hello," Ginny welcomed them to her aerial perch.

"We had a call about a woman on the roof writing 'Help!'" Officer Dewey panted, catching his breath from his hurried ascent.

Ginny indicated for them to follow her over the pitch of the roof, and pointed to her carefully painted letters: HELLO   FRANK

"My husband and friends are taking a Kenmore Air ride this morning. I know they'll come over the house. I wanted to say hi and surprise them."

115

"The house is all clear!" a voice shouted from the front yard.

"Oh," Officer Dewey said. "You must have just started when a private pilot went over low and became concerned. Glad there's no problem. We weren't sure what we might find."

"Cats on the roof are probably more common than seventy-three-year old grandmas?"

"Right," the fireman spoke. "Well, let's get you down. I'll go first, then Officer Dewey here can help you get on the ladder. We'll take it slow and easy."

"We could do that," Ginny said. "Or," she pointed to the back corner of the roof, "we could walk down the circular staircase my husband installed from our little bedroom deck. Easy roof access to clean the gutters."

Having been concentrating on the woman-in-peril call, both men had missed that detail or even stopped to wonder how Ginny had gotten on the roof in the first place. Officer Dewey escorted Ginny down the stairs and went on through the house, while the fireman, whose boots, Ginny had pointed out, were rather muddy from the yard, went back down his own ladder.

Reconnoitering in the front yard with her neighbor Caroline and several others who had come to see what the commotion was, everyone had a good laugh as Ginny thanked the officers and firemen for the quick response. She was a little anxious to get everyone on their way, just in case her thrill-seeking trio flew over the house right after takeoff. She had hoped to be sitting out front in a lawn chair reading a book when they went overhead.

"Smells great in here!" Frank boomed from the back door. "Brownies?"

"Yes. How was the trip?" She embraced her husband, happy to have him home safely.

"I thought," he held her shoulders and looked into her eyes seriously, "we had agreed not to be up on the roof alone?"

"I wasn't alone, actually. I had more company than I expected."

Paul and Joan entered then, and listened to Ginny's recounting of her morning interaction with the neighborhood before sharing their own experience in the air.

"It was a little scary to land," Joan admitted. "But really, very smooth."

"The scenery was gorgeous," Paul said. "We are so lucky to live here. And you should have heard Frank when we went over the house and he saw your sign. He said he was surprised it didn't say *Bring home some milk!*"

"I didn't even think of that. Might have saved some excitement, actually. Oh, well, I'm glad you had a good time. Now, I'm going to run these brownies over to the fire station. Oh, by the way," Ginny patted her husband's shoulder, "the guys thought the spiral staircase was brilliant. Wished every home had one!"

Chapter Twenty-Four

"Well, here we are again," Lindsay sat despondently beside her father in the ER.

"I know. I can't believe it," he replied. "One minute she was on her feet, the next, down she went, on a perfectly dry, warm, May evening."

"It was that crack in the sidewalk, she caught her foot," Ginny said, the vision of Joan stumbling and throwing out her hands to catch herself still fresh. "I knew right away it was broken, she had the most awful look on her face."

Lindsay's husband Mo appeared from the trauma rooms, where he had been stationed beside his mother from the minute he arrived. "She's okay," he said as Lindsay hugged him. "It's a simple fracture, but they'll wait to cast it tomorrow to let the swelling go down. They're splinting it now. She'll be ready to go home in about twenty minutes." He took a seat beside his in-laws.

"And her right arm, too," Ginny sighed. "She'll not be happy about that."

"I know," Mo agreed. "She's already complaining about it."

"We're lucky she didn't hit her head or break something else. Concrete is rather unforgiving," Frank said.

"Thanks for following the ambulance and driving Dad here. He's more shook-up than she is, actually. She's just mad," Mo warned them.

"Life is like that," Ginny said. "You're going along smoothly, and then wham!! A Brio train track or a sidewalk crack upends you completely." *Or a pregnancy, or job loss, or your kids aren't doing well....* Ginny pondered a host of other episodes in their lives. She patted

Mo's knee sympathetically. "Well, you know we'll take good care of her. I'm sure she'll have no trouble telling us what to do to be helpful."

"The doctor said she might be sore all over tomorrow, but it shouldn't be too bad. But she's to take it easy and keep her arm elevated to reduce the swelling."

"We'll help Paul take her to the doctor's tomorrow. It'll be easier with parking and all to have some extra hands."

"Thanks, I appreciate that," Mo said. "I have a meeting, but I could postpone it if there's any trouble overnight."

"I'm sure your dad will talk to you in the morning."

The doors to the waiting room opened and Paul appeared, pushing Joan in a wheelchair, her right arm in a sling.

"Here I am," Joan said gaily. "Making a grand entrance, as usual."

"Got some pain meds, did we?" Ginny asked with a raised eyebrow.

"Oh, yes, I'm feeling much better. Ready to go."

"Oh-kay," Frank drawled. "Let's get moving while she's feeling good. I'll get the car."

Mo took over the wheelchair, and the group made their way to the curb to await Frank.

"I'm so sorry, Mom," Lindsay planted a kiss on her mother-in-law's cheek. "What a scare it must have been."

"I'm fine," Joan replied. "Just angry at myself. I've walked on that sidewalk every day since we moved in. I don't know why my foot didn't clear the crack this time. It's so annoying. But it could have been worse. And it does get me out of dishes for at least six weeks!"

Mo tucked his mother tenderly into the back seat of the Jeep after Frank pulled up.

"Do you want us to go home with you?" Lindsay asked.

"I think I'll be fine," Joan replied. "I'm in good hands."

"We'll stop by tomorrow after work," Lindsay said.

Paul climbed into the back beside his wife, while Ginny took the front passenger seat.

Lindsay and Mo waved as the foursome pulled out. A long sigh escaped from Mo.

"We're lucky," Lindsay hugged him reassuringly as she watched their parents go. "They'll take good care of her, you know that."

"I know. I just...I always thought my mom was sort of invincible. She hardly even gets a cold or the flu anymore."

"I think the motor home debacle proved her immune system is solid iron. This little bump in the road doesn't mean we're entering the illness stage of their lives or anything. Falls happen."

"I guess." But seeing his mom on a triage table had unsettled Mo, his vision of the future turned ever so slightly in a different direction.

"Well, that was exciting," Joan said, settling in for the short ride home.

"How was the ambulance ride?" Ginny asked. "I found it much less comfortable than one would expect."

"It *was* bumpy. That surprised me. But they were very kind. I kept insisting I was a nurse, as if that had anything to do with anything. They probably thought I really had banged my head, I was so obnoxious about it."

Paul took his wife's good hand in his.

"You're awfully quiet," Joan said to her partner of over fifty years. "Hm?"

"What are you so quiet about?" Joan asked again.

"Oh, nothing. It all happened so fast, that's all. I was thinking that in all these years together, even with the boys, we've never had a broken bone. That's pretty lucky, I'd say."

"Really?" Frank voiced surprise from the driver's seat. "Even with the boys and sports? I think we've had at least three breaks that

120

I can remember: Pam's broken thumb, Lindsay's broken toe, and Robert's broken arm. And one concussion."

"We've been really lucky." Joan squeezed Paul's hand. "And that's not going to change. I promise."

"Here we are." Frank pulled up to the house.

Ginny was the first one out of the car. "Wait till I get the front light on. And watch out for the crack!"

Three mornings later Joan sat at the breakfast table, concentrating on making her left hand get the cereal on her spoon and into her mouth without making a mess. It was not as easy as she had expected. She heard her cell phone go off, and Ginny hopped up and brought it to her.

The others watched as Joan took the call, her face turning serious, and "Oh, dear," slipping out several times. Her reply included the news of her own broken arm, and that she'd have to check with her friends and then call back.

"Big Grandmas," she told the expectant crew. "Emergency."

"What kind?" Ginny asked.

"A new mom with a preemie just went down with pneumonia at home. And she has twin two-year-old boys. The baby was a month early and has only been home two weeks. They just got her off the feeding tube but she still uses some oxygen. The mom's parents can come from Los Angeles, but they won't get here till late Friday; they're going to bring their car and drive up so they can stay awhile. So that's four days away."

Ginny glanced at the big wall calendar they kept in the kitchen. She had Duplicate on Wednesday night. The rest of the week looked flexible.

"What if we all do it together? Would that work?"

"I think so. Her husband can come home a little early, and some friends can help in the evenings, but they still need about seven hours a day. Are you willing?"

The guys agreed to rise to the challenge of the two-year-old twins, while Ginny and Joan cared for the baby and mom. Joan called back and got the necessary information, and in another hour they were packed up and ready to go.

It was a small house on a cul-de-sac, twenty minutes from their home.

An exhausted father met them at the door, a crying newborn in his arms and a toddler hanging on each leg. After quick introductions, the four went to work, with Paul and Frank distracting the boys with blocks in the living room while Joan met Tricia, the ill mother. Ginny took the baby into the nursery and sat in the rocker, slowly soothing her to sleep. She was tinier than any of her own had been, but her good color and robust crying did not indicate any immediate oxygen requirement.

Adam, the father, showered and dressed for work. Joan checked out the kitchen situation. Friends had already started bringing food. The young mother was the most worried about keeping up her breast milk, since the baby had finally started nursing well after her two weeks in the hospital with a feeding tube.

When Adam returned at dinner time, his home was peaceful with the kitchen cleaned, the mountain of dirty laundry attended to, the little boys playing with their new big friends, and a delicious smell emanating from the oven. A friend had dropped by late afternoon, bringing dinner for an army and helping with the tidying up and laundry. Invited to stay and eat, the entire group enjoyed the lasagna, salad, and bread. Afterward, Ginny helped get the little ones into their pajamas and ready for bed, then Paul and Frank each read them some books. By seven o'clock the four grandparents-in-action were on their way home, ready to drop into bed themselves.

Tuesday went well after a few early tantrums from the boys over toys and not being allowed to bother their mother. Ginny spent most of her time with the baby, tiptoeing in and out of the master bedroom to check on her little charge who was sleeping in a bassinet near mom. After each feeding Ginny brought the baby to the nursery. She decided a comfortable rocker with a newborn sleeping on her chest was probably as close to heaven on earth as she was ever going to get.

They drove two cars on Wednesday, because Paul and Frank said they had an errand to do. They arrived forty minutes later, a huge box strapped to the roof of the car. *What on earth is that?* Ginny wondered, observing them from the nursery window.

The little boys were beside themselves with excitement, and crawled all over the men as they carried in the box and put it in the living room.

"A climber?" Ginny wandered in, looking at the box picture. "Inside?"

"These little guys have a lot energy. Their dad said it was okay, and I don't really think Tricia will care, do you?"

Thus, over the next hour, a rather large Little Tykes fort and climber with a slide, hiding places, and climbing footholds, took shape in the middle of the living room.

"Is it safe?" Ginny asked. "For two-year-olds?"

"It says ages two to six," Frank answered from his prone position on the floor, tightening a bolt.

"I think it's as safe as them jumping off the back of the couch, which has been happening non-stop the last two days every time we turn our backs," Paul added.

"I'll take that," Ginny retrieved a wrench from a pair of sticky little hands. "Let's go have our snack in the kitchen and let the big boys finish your climber, okay?"

"Very impressive," Joan admired her husband and friend's handiwork when she appeared an hour later, after giving one-handed help to Tricia who enjoyed a shower and hair wash. The twins were taking turns climbing up and sliding down the short slide, giggling with glee. Then they started sending their stuffed animals down the slide one at a time, and raced to their bedroom for more. Next came the cars and trucks racing downhill, then balls, then books, then pillows off the couch.

More friends arrived late afternoon, and Joan assigned one of them to try to organize the food in the refrigerator and make some kind of email list to get the helpers a little more organized.

The fourth day went fantastically well, with Tricia making her first foray through the house after lunch and sitting on the couch to read to her boys for fifteen minutes before returning to bed, exhausted.

"I can't thank you enough," she said to Ginny and Joan later that afternoon. "I don't know what we would have done. Adam was already so tired before I got sick, this would have sunk us. His parents flew in and kept the boys while we were spending our days at the hospital after Alyssa was born, and my parents were here for two weeks helping when we brought her home from the hospital. They had just flown home and then I got sick. That's why they needed a few days before turning around and coming back up." The tired mother lay back on her pillow and closed her eyes. "I can't believe what bad luck this is. But at least Alyssa is nursing now, that helps a lot."

"And you're getting stronger each day," Joan encouraged her. "But it's a long haul, you know. Six weeks maybe before you're back at full strength. So let people help you as much as you can. You try to take care of yourself and keep the milk going for Alyssa. She's getting stronger each day, too. I can tell just since we've been here."

On Friday afternoon, the cavalry arrived, with not only the grandparents, but the grandmother's sister, also, conscripted from San Francisco on the drive up from LA. The boys were overjoyed to see their grandparents again, and the grandparents, in turn, expressed heartfelt appreciation for all that had been done for their family.

On Saturday, Ginny woke up, realized there was no urgency to get out of bed, and rolled back over for more sleep. Unsuccessful, she found her place on Frank's chest.

"I miss that baby," she whispered to Frank, who was also enjoying not needing to spring into action with little ones today.

"That's because you got to spend your days sitting and rocking Alyssa. My back, however, is killing me. One more day lifting the boys would have done me in, I think."

"Oh, you loved every minute, don't try to fool me."

"I did like reading books to the little guys before nap time. That was my favorite." Frank was quiet for a few minutes. "Maybe we can go check on them sometimes. You know, just to be sure they're doing okay."

"Yes," Ginny patted his chest. "Just to be sure they're doing okay." Her eyes closed and she fell back asleep, not waking up until a workman's truck with a bad muffler rumbled by an hour later.

Chapter Twenty-Five

Paul sat on the patio, the May sun warming his back as he read an article in his professional magazine about the sorry state of pastors' pensions. He sighed. He and Joan were luckier than most, as she had worked as a nurse for most of their marriage. His parishioners had not had the benefit of the extra pastoral care given by so many pastor's wives of that era who willingly joined in their husband's ministries, but he and Joan were certainly more financially secure in their older years than many of his compatriots for whom the recession was decimating their retirement funds. And the last fifteen years before he retired he had been a tenured professor teaching Old Testament, so that dependable and steady income had helped immensely.

Ginny flitted by, dressed in her gardening pants and shirt, carrying three sizes of clippers and aiming for the next errant bush in the yard.

For the first few years that Paul and Joan had lived in an apartment after downsizing, Paul had not missed yardwork at all. Mowing, clipping, forever trying to keep blackberries and morning glory in check even in their small yard...he had missed none of it. But after a while, once Lindsay and Mo were married and he and Joan spent significant time celebrating events here at this house with Ginny and Frank, seeing their yard go through various seasons brought out some yearning in him. His wife had no patience for watching plants grow, but he found a certain joy in the daily change.

"Hey, Ginny," he called, saving a moderate limb from being decimated. "Let's make a big garden this year. Vegetables and flowers. A little bit of everything. Maybe even some new raised beds. I bet Frank could knock them out in no time."

Ginny put down her tools and came back to sit by Paul, claiming a sip of cold water. "What brought this on, Paul? It's a lot of work. I thought you didn't miss gardening."

"I didn't at first. But now I'd love to help you plant and grow things this summer. What do you think?"

"I'm all for it, of course. I've been planting less and less each year because Frank doesn't really enjoy it. He has enough to do mowing the lawn."

"What if we make his job a little less back here by putting in some raised beds?"

"What's your definition of raised?"

"Like two feet." Paul walked to the sunniest part of the backyard. "Right here. We could make three beds, 10 feet by three, and two feet high."

"That would take a lot of soil to fill…60 cubic feet each…isn't that over 7 cubic yards all together?"

"We'll get a load delivered and have all the kids over to help shovel. Make an afternoon of it. It'll be fun."

Ginny smiled. Now this was the kind of fun she liked to have.

And thus was born what came to be known as the 2010 Gardening Project, or "The Project" for short.

Two weeks later, Frank had built the beds, the soil had been delivered and all the kids and grandkids had been pressed into service. There was enough soil left over from the 10 cubic yard delivery to top dress all the beds around the house. Ginny was thrilled as the rich soil covered her worn and weary patches of earth. Joan helped by catering a hearty dinner of Chinese take-out for the tired workers, served at the picnic table on the patio since it had rained most of the day and muddy clothes were the most common element among the crew.

Next, Ginny took Paul to the nursery to buy plants and seeds.

"Do we have a budget?" Paul asked as he surveyed the expansive botanical beauty before him.

"I think we already spent the wad on the raised beds and soil."

"Well, you take a cart for the flowers, and I'll take one for the vegetables."

It was two hours before Ginny could pull Paul away, and it was mostly because they had filled four carts, and he had also picked up one of every kind of vegetable seed packet.

"Just for fun," he kept saying, as he grabbed sweet pea and wildflower seeds. "And giant Jack-o-lanterns, of course. We can grow them at the end of the lawn by the fence. Won't Alex and the little girls love them? Oh, look at this poster about ladybugs. We can get some later, right?"

Disappointed that it was too early to plant tomatoes, as the nights were too cool, Paul caught sight of a simple greenhouse structure with a hefty price tag. "I bet Frank could build one for a quarter of this price," he told Ginny as he tested its sturdiness. "Then we could start things from seeds instead of having to buy plants. That would save money." He smiled at her encouragingly.

Ginny paused. This was her chance, here was help, *real* help, with real ideas, and sincere enthusiasm. Why *not* take advantage of it?

"Yes, that's a great idea," she agreed, having no idea she had greenlighted much more than a plastic and wood slat edifice.

Paul's "great idea" morphed exponentially from the small greenhouse, to a lovely garden shed with a greenhouse attached on the sunny side, to more of a cottage shape with a potting bench, front porch, and a spacious greenhouse attached. ("The cottage will be a great place for the teens to hang out," Paul declared.) And when the three youngest grandchildren caught wind of the construction, they requested a small playhouse for themselves.

Meanwhile, Joan kept track of the expenses:
   Wood for raised beds
   Soil
   New wheelbarrow
   Plants and seeds
   Greenhouse materials
   Cottage and potting bench
   Playhouse
   Expected cost per carrot grown in the first season: $500

Ginny watched contentedly from inside as Frank and Paul laid the flooring in the shed-turned-cottage. No matter the yield of their first-year crop, the amount of lawn for Frank to mow had been sizably reduced. Surely he would be happy about that!

Chapter Twenty-Six

This time it was Frank at the table in late May, looking at his AAA travel magazine.

"What about going to Sequoia National Park?" he said to the others, who were in various stages of working the newspaper brainteasers.

"Sequoia?" Ginny asked. "Why there?"

"It's fantastic," Joan said, looking up from her Sudoku. "We went years and years ago. The trees...I can't do them justice. If you've never been, then we must go."

"Let's pack up and go!" Paul agreed. Now that the backyard construction and planting were complete, he was ready for adventure again. "I'll get an RV, we can be on our way next week!"

"Reservations?" Ginny mentioned. "Wouldn't that be a good idea? It's nearly summer."

"That's the joy of an RV," Paul said. "You've got your bed with you. But I'll check into things and see what I can get."

"What about the garden? We've just spent all that time putting in the seeds and new plants." Ginny had been spending at least an hour each day tenderly caring for the young sprouts and seedlings.

"No problem. Lindsay and Mo can bring the kids over, and we'll pay them to water," Paul said, unfamiliar with both the intricacies of fragile new plants and the inconsistencies of his grandchildren's schedules. "Win, win."

It did take a week to get their plans confirmed, but soon the two couples were on their way, with abundant promises from Lindsay to keep the gardens, which had all sprouted energetically under the lengthening days and Ginny's green thumb, well-watered.

Upon further consideration, Paul had decided that they wouldn't take the medium-sized RV he had reserved up the curvy switchbacks to the park's 1700 foot entrance. He had found a motel down below in Visalia where they could park the rig for the week, then take a rental car up to the national park. For their park lodging, he had secured the last available cabin at the Lodgepole campground for five nights.

The drive through Oregon to California was uneventful. They chose to drive the less picturesque I-5 south, and then return home by way of US 101, the scenic coastal highway, so that they could return to Washington on the inside lane going north. Paul had a few bad memories of driving US 101 south along the steep drop-offs in their tiny old Toyota, unable to enjoy the view because he couldn't take his eyes from the road. Experiencing the drive going north, clinging to the mountain side rather than the cliffs, made much more sense.

They spent one night in Visalia, then secured their rental car and prepared to make their way up into Sequoia National Park.

"Take water," the motel clerk reminded them. "It's pretty dry up there."

"Good idea," Paul said. They made their first stop at a little market where they each bought a quart size water bottle to drink for the day.

The switchbacks were making Ginny nauseous in the back seat of the comfortable Toyota Camry. She tried to find a point on the horizon on which to focus, but the forest growth did not help. When she thought she couldn't stand it another minute, they broke through into blue sky. They pulled into the visitor's center so they could all stretch their legs and use the rest room. Already Ginny could feel the difference in the air.

"How high is the park?" she asked Paul.

131

"I think the area around the Giant Forest is about 6,400 feet, if I remember correctly. The Sierra peaks range all the way up to Mount Whitney. It's over 14,500 feet, so a little higher than Mount Rainier. But you can't see Whitney from the park, you've got to look from its other side."

Paul got directions and they made their way to their accommodations, a few cabins at the back of the Lodgepole campgrounds. They pulled up in front of a natural-looking structure with a front porch, and the sound of water gently rushing nearby.

"Oh, it's adorable!" Joan exclaimed, key in her uncasted left hand and the first one out of the car and up the steps to the porch.

Ginny followed, but after unlocking the door, Joan took one step in and stopped abruptly.

"What's wrong?" Ginny asked, nearly knocking into her.

"Paul, are you sure this is the right one?" Joan called to her husband.

"Yep. Why?"

"Well," Joan moved aside so Ginny could see. "It's…it's…pretty rustic."

Two double beds with bright quilts lined each wall, then a picnic table with benches in the front corner by the door. Four straight-backed chairs around a fire place.

"No kitchen," Ginny called over her shoulder.

"No bathroom," Joan added.

By this time Paul was up the stairs with a suitcase.

"Hmm," he pondered. "Let me see." He pulled out his reservation form, matching the number with the carved number on the wooden door. "It's definitely the one I signed up for. I guess it might have been described as "basic" or "rustic" or something like that. I didn't really read the fine print on all the differences. There were only a few cabins available here in Sequoia, and all but this one were taken. Most of the cabins are over in Kings Canyon, farther in. Hmm."

Frank had made a short trip around the campground loop. "The common bathrooms are just a hundred yards down the road. We're pretty close."

Ginny looked at her three companions. "I'm not going down that road in the middle of the night. First thing, we need to find a store and buy a bucket."

"You can wake me and I'll go with you after dark," Frank offered.

"I'm with Ginny on this one," Joan said. "We don't even have a flashlight."

With that all four had the same realization and looked up to see if there were any lights.

"No electricity, either, I guess. I'd say *rustic* sums it up quite well," Joan observed.

"No wonder you could get the reservation last minute," Ginny commented dryly. "That should have been our first clue."

"It'll be fine. An adventure," Frank cajoled her. "Let's unpack, then we'll find the store and a place to eat."

Walking to the camp store and small restaurant, Ginny could tell they were woefully unprepared compared to most people who were either car camping or had their RVs, each setting up full kitchens at their camp sites. Luckily, there was a well-stocked store where they purchased flashlights, some gallons of water, a bucket, matches, and new ice for their ice chest, which only contained some orange juice and lunch meat. At least they had brought the proper clothing, Ginny thought. Being early June, the breeze was cool, and she zipped her light-weight jacket up a bit higher.

After a late lunch, they returned to their cabin for a rest. Once they were refreshed, they set out on a short hike that followed the campground creek.

133

Dinner at the restaurant was next. A simple menu offered tasty and filling choices that left them needing a stroll through the various campground loops. Back on the porch, they pulled the four chairs out and sat, watching the campers go about their evening duties. With the setting sun they turned in, each reading in bed a bit before turning out their flashlights.

A loud middle-of-the-night thump and crash on the porch woke all of them from deep sleep.

"What WAS that?" Ginny asked.

Paul went to the door with his flashlight, shining the beam out the glass.

"Black bear," he said. "Pretty big. Um, where's our cooler? Inside, right?"

"No," Ginny said from under the covers where she fully intended to stay. "I set it outside to help it stay cold."

"Oh, that's it then. These bears all know that a cooler means food. He probably just toppled it and is enjoying the turkey right now. We'll deal with it in the morning."

"I'm sorry," Ginny apologized. "I knew you shouldn't leave food out. I just wasn't thinking that they could smell it through the cooler. All the other campsites had their coolers out, I thought it was safe."

"They probably lock them in their cars at night. No harm done." Paul said, settling back into bed.

Ginny pulled the covers up even higher. "I'm not moving till daylight."

They all woke a little stiff from the old mattresses and small beds. But energized by coffee and a good breakfast, they set out for their day's adventure: Moro Rock, a giant dome of granite made accessible by 400 steps and accompanying railings rising 300 feet to the top.

"Think our knees are up to the challenge?" Paul asked them at the bottom. "It's fantastic once you get there. And we can go as slowly as you like. We'll all have sore knees tomorrow, but this is the hardest hike we'll take."

They agreed to try, Ginny the most reluctant. "Maybe I'll stop halfway up and wait for you," she said, eyeing the narrow path, multitude of stairs, and large admonition about being struck by lightning. "Just reading this sign is making the hair on the back of my neck stand up," she said.

Paul and Joan went in front, since they had been there before. Frank followed Ginny, in a gallant effort to bring up the rear. The narrow path of steps required concentration, but each time Ginny paused and looked up from her feet, she was overcome with awe as the mountain ranges unfolded before her.

Once at the top of the rounded dome, the whisper of sound was one she'd never heard before. Not wind, exactly. Something bigger, like the background noise of something immense and unimaginable. A sound that had been there since the beginning. It made Ginny feel very insignificant in the overall scheme of things. She liked the feeling.

The view of the High Sierras and Great Western Divide was breathtaking. Ginny lingered when the others were ready to go and they had to call her several times.

"It's wonderful," was all she could say.

That evening they sat out in the dark and watched the stars for half an hour. Ginny and Frank had never seen the heavens in the absence of city light. Paul pointed out the most concentrated swath of stars as the Milky Way. An occasional shooting star streaked across part of the sky before blinking out, and they all took turns pointing out the most familiar constellations. Then as the campers around them quieted, the four tired hikers also retreated to their lightless cabin.

Now snuggled under the covers and plastered beside Frank, all Ginny could see when she closed her eyes was the magnificent vista of the afternoon. She fell asleep after reading only four pages, and Frank tenderly removed her book and glasses, and turned off her flashlight, which had fallen from her hand onto the quilt.

"What IS that?" Joan shot straight up in bed as the sound of a jackhammer filled the cabin at dawn.

Ginny listened to the loud pounding. "I bet it's a pileated woodpecker. Listen to the rhythm." She pulled a sweatshirt on over her nightgown and went out the front door, straining to follow the sound in the tree heights, but she couldn't find what she was searching for: a 15-inch, black and white master driller with a red crest. The sound was unmistakable, and Ginny was disappointed when the pounding stopped and she had not gotten even a peek.

Ginny was beginning to enjoy her foray to the restroom in the mornings, taking care of their overnight bucket potty, splashing cold water on her face, and brushing her teeth. There were moms with kids trying to do sink baths, others washing dishes, and some simply trying to have a moment alone in the stalls while keeping in verbal contact with little ones on the other side of the door.

Paul's schedule for the day began with visiting the Giant Forest Museum, and then walking through the Giant Forest itself. When the girth of the first giant sequoia tree came into view, Ginny came to a full stop, stunned to speechlessness. She craned her head back, trying to see the top, but only massive limbs filled the uppermost space. It simply took her breath away to be in the midst of such massive, living, *beings*.

Frank read to her from the sign of the tree named The President: third largest tree, 247 feet high, 23 feet in diameter.

Ginny touched the feathery bark, rested her hand on the trunk, and closed her eyes. She thought she could feel the pulse of the tree beneath her fingertips. She listened to the wind blowing softly through this forest of giants, and became completely overwhelmed.

"This tree is 3200 years old," Frank informed her. "I think that's the Bronze Age or something. Way before Jesus."

Ginny placed her ear against the colossal tree trunk, as if listening for a heartbeat. The others looked at her curiously.

"You okay, honey?" Frank inquired, unsure of his wife's attachment to the tree.

"I am," Ginny whispered and hugged the tree. "I love these trees," she turned and looked at her friends. "I want to stay here forever. I want to see all of them. I want to see every big tree in the park. In California. Maybe in America."

"That's going to put a few more pages on the bucket list," Paul said, stepping back to take a picture. "Smile, Ginny!"

It would become one of her favorite pictures, hung on the kitchen wall, capturing the moment when she became a traveler.

"So your mom had a good time?" Tess inquired of Lindsay in their first conversation after the Sequoia explorers returned to civilization.

"She loved it. She didn't even care that she didn't get a shower for almost a week. Dad said once she got her hands on those big trees, she was a changed woman. Unreal. Now she wants to see every big tree in America. She's making a list of heritage trees all over the West Coast."

"I suppose it fits with her love of nature. No one ever got her matched up with the right destination before, I guess. How'd she take the garden news?"

Lindsay sighed and grabbed one bag of groceries from the car and headed to her front door. "I think Paul was actually the most disappointed. Who knew we were going to have such a hot spell right when they were gone? I guess we didn't water deeply enough or something, I don't know. Mom thought she could save the tomatoes and beans. The lettuce and half the flowers are toast, though. Alex got paid for the half that lived through the trauma, so he's thrilled. But I think Joan's accounting of cost per carrot just went up again…assuming they get a single carrot to harvest!"

Chapter Twenty-Seven

On Saturday, learning from Mo that Lindsay was at her mother's, Tess knocked twice on the Noonan's front door, then opened it and entered without waiting for an invitation, as she had done ever since she and Lindsay became best friends in second grade.

Lindsay looked up from her seat at the kitchen table, and Ginny paused in cutting the brownies she had pulled from the oven an hour before.

"What's wrong?" they said together in concern, as the tearful Tess plopped into a chair and buried her head in her hands and sobbed.

"Tess, darling, what is it?" Ginny hugged her shoulders tenderly. "Betty?"

Tess nodded, trying to gain control.

"I just saw her on Monday. She showed me around the place…it's not so bad. I thought maybe she even liked it." Ginny patted the shoulder of this girl who was like another daughter to her.

"She hates it," Tess sniffled.

"But it's just the transition. She'll get used to it, don't you think?" Lindsay reached for some tissues for her friend.

"This morning," Tess said softly, barely able to complete the sentence, "this morning she snuck away from the outdoor group, called a cab, and went up to the casino. She'd only been there an hour, hadn't even been missed yet at the center, when she fainted. They took her to the hospital and then back to 'the brig' as she calls it. Along with a hefty cabulance bill."

"Is she all right?"

"She's fine. Well, as fine as you can be with worsening emphysema and heart failure. She hadn't eaten, was all. But the administrator said if she does it again they'll either have to medicate her or kick her out. They can't have people running off all over the place not telling them."

"But she's not on a locked unit, though, is she?" Lindsay asked.

"No. But you're still supposed to check in and out. And, technically, she's supposed to be on her last legs and bed-ridden. I don't know where she got the strength to slip away from the group. They were out enjoying the sun in the rear garden. She'd obviously managed to scope out the back gate and arrange for a cab to get her to the casino bus stop. She's incorrigible."

"Well, that's too bad," Ginny sympathized. "I thought she was doing so well through her garage sale and all. It's not easy to have to jettison all your possessions."

"I just don't know what to do," Tess wiped her eyes. "She can't live with me. There's not room, and I'd probably kill her within the first week. She still hasn't stopped smoking, so that was the other thing. She slides out for a smoke whenever she can. I don't even know where she gets the cigarettes. She probably has half the staff on the take to buy them for her."

"Could you talk to the casino? Ask them to deny her entrance?"

"Are you kidding? She's one of their favorite customers. They love her. She's dropped so much money up there, they'd let her roll in in her hospital bed, I think."

"I'm sorry, Tess," Ginny brought her a brownie. "Here, this will help. What more can you do? It's the best assisted living and nursing care in town. It seemed like a good choice."

"The doctor told her to get her affairs in order. She's had a long run with these diseases, and at some point her luck is going to end. She gets so breathless she practically turns blue, but she refuses to wear the oxygen except at night. It's like she couldn't even hear what he was saying."

"We'll think of something," Ginny consoled her. "We'll think of something. Maybe Frank can talk some sense into her."

Lying in bed two days later, the idea in Ginny's mind that had started percolating during her visit to check on the miserable Betty finally came into full vision.

"What if," Ginny patted Frank's chest as she lay against him, to be sure he was fully awake. "What if we brought Betty here to live? Just for a month? Until she's, you know, so close to the end she's a little more manageable?"

"You're crazy," Frank said with no hesitation. "How exactly are *we* going to manage her? And where would we put her?"

"She won't need to be managed if she's happy. She's just so unhappy there, she's lost all control of everything, and you know how hard that was for us to even think about. And we were still independent enough to get out and about. With some squeezing, I think we could get a hospital bed into the den if we take out the couch. The bathroom's right there, although she'd have to go upstairs to shower or bathe."

"The smoking."

"Yes. That would be the condition. She absolutely has to stop. Maybe a patch or med or something. She has to have stopped for two weeks before we'll even consider it. I think she'd do it."

"What about Paul and Joan?"

"What about them? We took them in, didn't we? I can't imagine they'd mind. They've known Betty almost as long as we have."

Frank sighed, searching in vain for a reason this idea wouldn't work, beyond all the obvious red flags that his wife would have an answer to.

"It means Tess will be over here all the time. And her kids."

"We love Tess. And her kids."

"She HAS to stop smoking."

"I already said that."

"And it's conditional. If it doesn't work out, I want a backup plan figured out and agreed to before she sets foot in the door."

"Frank, all this negativity. I'm surprised at you." Ginny hoisted herself on her elbow to look clearly at her husband.

"I'm sorry, but she's not the easiest person to get along with, do you think? We're all doing so well right now, I don't want to upset the apple cart." Frank searched his wife's face earnestly.

"We're not talking about forever," Ginny sank back down on his chest. "Let's ask Joan, but I don't think it will be long before she hits her final decline. Two months or less at the rate she's going, is what Tess said after their last doctor's visit."

"Isn't it awkward to be hoping for someone's final decline?"

"You're being impossible now, do you know that?"

Frank was silent for a few moments, considering all options. "Okay, here it is. Paul and Joan have to wholeheartedly agree. Betty has to quit smoking for two weeks, no cheating, and she can't bring any of her stinky, smoked-filled possessions here. Has to get new clothes, everything. And we have a backup plan for now, and for later, if she needs heavy care. I don't want you and Joan doing that. A hospice place or something."

"Agreed."

After a few moments of silence, Frank said, "I bet Paul can help her get her finances in order."

Ginny smiled and patted his chest again.

"But what about your bucket list? What about your plan to visit all the Big Trees?" Lindsay wanted to know when her mother broke the news.

"Don't worry. The trees will all still be there. They've made it this long, right?"

It didn't take much to get the den ready for Betty's arrival, since she was bringing very little. All of her smoke-infused possessions now resided in a storage unit leased by Tess. Her few new clothes, and even a new purse, containing a check-book with a new leather cover, passed Frank's sniff test as she was wheeled in and tucked into the hospital bed which now took center stage in the den. Frank's desk still fit in the corner, and a bookcase had been cleared under the window. A sitting chair brought from the living room made the room look cozy. The oxygen concentrator nestled beside the lampstand, tucked out of sight. Ginny had cleared enough out of the closet to hang the new clothes, and they'd bought a plastic four-drawer unit that also fit in the closet to hold Betty's underwear and nighties.

Tess fought back tears as she watched Joan and Ginny tenderly attend her mother. "Maybe this will work," she said to Lindsay from their viewpoint in the hall, out of the way. "It's just for a little while. Two months, max."

After her mother was settled in bed, Tess pulled the desk chair over and sat beside her. Betty was struggling with her breath, even with the oxygen, after the exertion of the move. She lay back on her elevated pillows and closed her eyes, her thin hand reaching for her daughter's.

"Oh, Tess. I'm sorry I smoked all those years. You tried so hard to help me quit. Writing CANCER STICK on all my packs when you were in elementary school, remember?"

Tess remembered all too well. There was a bit of a competition in her fifth grade class to see who could get their parents to quit. She had known she had little chance of winning, and probably couldn't even get an honorable mention in the "Cutting Back" category. "Well,

I'm just glad you quit," she told her mother. "Even if it was only two weeks ago."

"I was thinking heaven is probably non-smoking by now. Hell, too, maybe."

"Oh, Mom."

"Your father died first, you know, and he never smoked a day in his whole life."

"I know," Tess nodded. "But he drank an awful lot. I'm pretty sure that's where cirrhosis of the liver comes from."

"Occupational hazard."

Of what, Tess wondered, patting her mother's arm, letting her rest. Seeing her vulnerable and defenseless in a hospital bed instead of strolling through gardens with a cigarette dangling was a shock of reality Tess had thought she was prepared for, but apparently not. As her mother drifted off to sleep, Tess let her tears fall quietly, unrestrained, trying to imagine what she would do without her mother, impossible as she was.

Chapter Twenty-Eight

An unusual sound downstairs woke Frank, and he pulled on his robe to go investigate, discovering the patio door ajar and their patient sitting outside.

"What are you doing out here, Betty? It's 2 a.m."

"I couldn't sleep."

"You're not smoking, are you?" He sniffed the air suspiciously.

"No, don't worry. But I do miss it so."

"It's killing you, you idiot."

"I know. I've stopped. But it's so hard. I just needed to get out."

Frank pulled up a chair and sat beside Betty in the moonlight.

"I never wanted it to be this way, Frank. After her father died, I swore I'd make it easy on Tess. And I've tried. We just see things differently, that's all."

"Hey, I've got four kids, I understand that."

"I have not thanked you and the others properly for taking me in," Betty touched his arm lightly. "Really, I wouldn't have lasted another week in that place."

"It's the most expensive skilled nursing center in the city!"

"I know. But...it wasn't for me. I've really always spent a lot of my time outside."

"Smoking."

"Well, yes, that's true. But I need to be out and about. If I can't, I might as well pack it in." She attempted to take a deep breath of the night air to accentuate her point, but started a wracking, raggedy, coughing spell instead. Frank gently helped her back to bed.

"We're not going to have to put a GPS on you, are we?" he said, only half-kidding.

"I'm not sure. If you put a chair right there outside the patio door, I promise that's as far as I'll go."

"Deal."

Frank replaced the oxygen situated under her nose, waiting until he was sure she was resting comfortably before returning to his room.

The next day he rearranged the porch furniture with two chairs beside the patio door, under the overhang and protected from the weather. Betty spent the times when she was out of bed sitting there, bundled up even in the warm summer sun and under an umbrella if it was raining,

One unusually rainy morning a week after she'd moved in, Betty called Ginny to her side.

"Do you think we could take a little trip?"

"A trip?"

"I would love to go to the casino one last time. We'll take the wheelchair, we'll just go for an hour. The drive will be lovely this time of year."

"It's forty minutes straight up I-5. Not exactly fall trees turning colors in New England and we've already missed the spring tulip festival."

"I know. That was a stretch, maybe. But have you four ever been to a casino? It's fun. It would be good for you."

"I don't know, Betty. What would Tess say?"

"Tess would say, 'Do whatever she wants to do to get her off this earth in a happy mood.' "

"I doubt that. But I'll ask the others. When would you want to go?"

"How about after lunch? After your nap?"

146

"Today?"

"I figure you all have things to do this morning."

"We'll get in the late afternoon traffic."

"It's not that bad, believe me. And late afternoon is a good time at the casino... day players going home, the evening ones haven't arrived yet."

"Of course the traffic is bad. Unless we left by 2:00. What about going next week?"

Tess gave a dramatic cough. "I'm just afraid...you know... anything could happen."

Ginny shook her head. However, Betty had been there a week so far and hadn't requested anything other than the chair on the patio. She'd given up smoking cold turkey, was quiet, and helped as much she could with her own care.

Thus, after an early lunch and naps, the five of them, with the wheelchair in the back of the van and the portable oxygen in use on Betty, traveled to the largest northern casino, Betty's favorite. She was greeted warmly as they made their entrance.

Ginny, Frank, Paul, and Joan stood awkwardly in the mammoth room.

"Let's each agree, we'll get $50 in chips apiece. When we lose that, we're done. If you make some, put half of it aside and don't spend it. That way we might come out ahead enough to pay for the gas up here," Paul advised.

"Or pay for dinner. I've heard the restaurant is great," Joan added. "If Betty is holding up, maybe we could eat here." It was her and Paul's night to cook, so a lovely restaurant fifty feet away seemed an excellent option.

"What's the easiest thing to try, do you think?" Ginny asked.

"The slot machines are pure chance, so that's very simple. But if you want to think a little, maybe try blackjack," Paul suggested.

"Which table is it?"

147

"I'll take you over after we get our chips," Frank said, guiding his wife to the teller's cage. "Then I think I'll park at the roulette wheel."

"I'll do slots for a while," Joan said. "I mostly want to people watch."

"Speaking of which," Paul looked around until he spotted Betty. "Do you think I should stick with the patient?"

"I'd be very surprised if she's not in excellent hands," Frank responded.

"Okay. Shall we meet back here in about an hour?" Ginny asked.

"Sounds like a plan." After getting her chips, Joan first headed toward the restaurant to check out the menu.

Frank settled Ginny at the blackjack table, and talked her through the first few rounds, before moving to the roulette wheel.

Ginny tried to get comfortable. There were only two other players at the table, both women her age. Ginny observed them as she watched the next few rounds, trying to get a feel for the rhythm of the game.

An hour later, Paul, Joan, and Frank had reassembled at the meeting spot, but Ginny was still at the blackjack table. They were going to give her a hard time until they saw the stack of chips in front of her as they approached.

"Hey, love," Frank planted a kiss on the back of her head. "Looks like you're doing well!"

"Sh. I'm trying to concentrate."

Frank stood contritely and glanced at Joan, who shrugged her shoulders. They watched in silence as Ginny took the next two rounds and added to her pile.

"Time to go," Paul said quietly. "It's good to stop when you're ahead."

Ginny seemed to digest this information, then suddenly looked at her watch and came back to earth. She swiveled and smiled at her compatriots. "I LOVE this game!"

"Beginner's luck?" Paul asked the dealer.

"No, she's got a knack for it," he replied.

As they sat around the dinner table with Betty, Ginny related her good luck.

"It's the Duplicate," Betty finally said. "Forty years of counting cards in bridge, it just comes naturally to you. I used to do well, too, but now I can't keep the cards straight."

"You're right," Ginny looked at her with appreciation. "It felt so natural, like I was checking off numbers in my head. What a fun game."

"Did anyone else win at your table?" Frank asked.

"A little bit, not much. I think I'm the only one who won consistently."

"Who would have thought it?" Joan said. "You're the one who didn't even want to come."

"Going new places isn't all bad, I guess. And to prove it, I'll pick up the tab!"

It was a cheery group in the car on the ride home. Betty spoke about the various dealers with whom she had become friends, and how she thought she was pretty much breaking even, more or less, or at least not losing that much each time.

As Ginny tucked her in bed, Betty grabbed her hand.

"Thank you. Thank you so much. I had to get out and forget about all—" she waved her hand toward her meds and the oxygen cord, "this. For a little bit."

"Of course. Anytime. We're happy to go places with you, whenever you feel you're up to it."

Betty smiled contentedly, thinking that she would certainly like to beat the house once more before her time was up.

Chapter Twenty-Nine

On the first of August, Frank sat at his desk looking through junk mail. Sharing his former office space with Betty in her hospital bed had worked out better than he expected. She didn't interrupt him much when he was working, and she seemed to enjoy his quiet presence. Betty had been spending less time out of bed, made fewer trips to the back patio, and after one more trip to the casino, hadn't seemed interested in returning. She put down the mystery paperback she had been trying to read and gazed out the window at the sunny weather.

"Frank?"

"Hmm?" he tore his address off an advertisement for cemetery plots and put it in the trash before recycling the rest of the solicitation.

"How do you know when it's time to quit fixing things?"

"Fixing things? What things?"

"Like body things?"

Frank swiveled the chair to look at his friend. "What are you talking about?"

Betty sighed. "It's not that much fun lying here waiting to die, that's all. But getting up and going requires so much effort." A wracking cough punctuated the end of her sentence.

"How so?"

"My legs are so weak. My breathing is bad. My strength is slipping away."

"Might help if you ate a little more. And a little more healthfully."

"If you can't eat junk food on your death bed, then life really sucks."

Frank had noticed Betty's vocabulary of late seemed to match her deteriorating state, but he couldn't argue with her reasoning.

"I think you should make the effort to feel as good as you can while you're still of this earth, I guess."

"I could be at death's door this very moment. There's no way to tell what's coming around the bend."

"If you tried hospice again, I think they are clued into all those little changes that mean something."

"They didn't want me the first time, I'm not getting rejected again."

"You know it wasn't like that, Betty. As I recall, I believe *you* fired *them*. I think you weren't emotionally ready for all they offered. Now you've had a bit of an improvement after moving in with us. Quitting smoking and all that."

"I can't just lie here and melt into the sheets."

"Maybe Nurse Joan is the better one to be talking to about this, don't you think?"

"No, she's too cheery. You're the practical one of the group. I've always admired your approach to life."

Betty lay still for a few moments while Frank went back to the junk mail.

"I've been thinking about getting a physical therapist," she broke the silence.

Now Frank's attention turned to her again. "What?"

"I heard of a holistic physical therapist who works with older people. I thought I might inquire."

"What does 'holistic' mean in this context?" Frank had always been confused about whether the word came from "holy" or from "whole." And if it *was* from "whole," why wasn't it spelled "wholistic"?

"I think they look at the entire situation, you know. Kind of understand where you are and where you're going. Absolute physical perfection might not be the goal."

"Sounds interesting. Would you need to go through your doctor for a referral?"

"Probably. But I was thinking of doing it as private pay. Once you get the insurance involved it seems to take the fun out of it. But I'm afraid Tess would think I'm crazy."

"That's not true."

"It is. She's been expecting my quiet and remorseful demise for years."

"Only because you've seemed quite ill. Your cough alone clears a room in ten seconds."

"Yes, well, there is that." And a wracking cough sealed the point.

Frank considered. Paul was the one helping Betty with her finances, and he had been mum on what her financial worries might be. "If you can afford it, then why not?"

"That's what I was thinking. Even a few sessions might make it easier to get out of bed a little more."

"Then go for it," Frank said. "If you can't have physical therapy when you're on your deathbed, then life *really* sucks."

"Thanks, Frank. You're a good friend." She was quiet for a moment before adding, "I don't know if *I* would have been brave enough to bring a stranger into my home to die."

"Well, you're hardly a stranger, and there's four of us to help, that makes a big difference. And you've been a pretty easy houseguest so far. Hopefully, I won't regret this conversation."

Betty picked up her mystery, determined to make some calls the next day. Frank finished sorting the mail and went out to help Ginny

153

start dinner. He decided not to mention the conversation, and wait till Betty brought it up to the others herself.

"She's doing what?" Lindsay asked Tess the next day during their late afternoon conversation.

"She's getting physical therapy. She heard of a holistic kind of person who will come to the house."

"Are you upset about it?"

"Not upset, just surprised, I guess. I don't know what she's expecting to accomplish. She's refused to go to the doctor or let the visiting nurse come check her. She's still mad about the hospice thing. I didn't handle that well, I guess." Tess rubbed her forehead in painful memory of the episode. "She got so angry about all the people involved. Any normal person would be delighted to have so much care available, but not *my* mother. Oh no. She doesn't want anyone to see her but good old Dr. Keiffer, not that she ever really listened to him."

"I don't think anyone really goes gently into the night, Tess. I remember my grandparents, and it was a bumpy ride at the end."

"But your folks have been so kind to take her in. I don't want any trouble."

"They can all stick up for themselves. I know your mom's been a handful at times before this, but things seem good over there. Kind of gives them all a focus, a project to work on together." Lindsay hated to admit it, but despite her initial reservations about the new arrangement, she was secretly and selfishly pleased that her parents' and in-laws' travels had been momentarily curtailed and they were back on the babysitting circuit.

"I guess we'll see what happens. I mean, the doctor said she could take a downturn anytime." Even though Tess repeated the phrase often, she did not fully believe that her mother's life was coming to an end.

"Try not to worry. Enjoy the time you have."

"Easier said than done," Tess sighed.

"I know. I'm sorry."

"Well, time to start dinner."

"Okay. Talk to you tomorrow." Lindsay sat in the car for another moment before gathering her things and bracing for her second job at home.

Chapter Thirty

Ginny was straightening Betty's bed while Betty sat in the chair in the morning sunlight.

"Have you ever played golf?" Betty asked out of the blue.

"Me?" Ginny straightened up. "No. I mean, some miniature golf with the kids a few times. I don't think I've been out on a real golf course in my whole life. Why?"

"I've been feeling so much better. The physical therapy is working, my legs are much stronger."

"After only a week?"

"Really, they are. Frank and Paul play, don't they? How about Joan?"

"Frank used to play occasionally. He still has his clubs. Paul and Joan probably play the most; they would play on their vacations, I think. Why?"

"I'd like to go play, one last time. I was quite a golfer, you know. Won the Ladies' Championship a few times in my day."

"I guess I do remember Tess mentioning that…a long time ago. Have you played since George died?"

"No. And I miss it."

Ginny finished the bed and was about to leave.

"Let's go play," Betty blurted out. "This afternoon. The five of us. The weather is perfect, no rain in sight the weatherman said."

Ginny was confused about her patient. Was a dementia component setting in?

"You want to go play golf, today."

"Obviously, I won't be able to do much. Maybe just putt a little bit. It would feel so wonderful to get out in the air, in nature. I think it would be good for me. I'll bring my portable oxygen, just in case. This might be my last chance. We'll take carts!"

Ginny, despite being incredibly kind-hearted, was becoming slightly suspicious of the "last chance" reasoning that had fueled the casino trips, two late night drives for ice cream cones, a sleepover with Betty's grandsons in sleeping bags around her bed, a steady stream of old friends visiting for the last time, and now golfing.

Yet as the afternoon was clear of other commitments, and the weather cooperative, the foursome decided to indulge Betty and go attempt nine holes and see how far they could get. Paul pulled Betty's walker from the corner.

"I won't need that," Betty said emphatically.

"For stability," Joan said, in her best nursing voice.

"I've got the four of you, I don't need that thing. Somebody bring the oxygen." And with that Betty got her jacket and headed to the van on Frank's arm.

At the golf course, Betty was greeted warmly by the manager at the uncrowded course. "It's been some time," he said to her kindly.

"I know, I haven't played since George died. Now I'm on my deathbed, and I wanted to see the course one more time. My good friends here are indulging me."

Ginny cast a glance at Joan, whose eyebrow had raised at what was becoming a familiar deathbed refrain. Betty insisted on paying for everyone, and soon they were set up in three carts with rented clubs for Betty and Ginny.

"We'll be together," Betty took Ginny's arm conspiratorially. "It'll be fun."

"I haven't ever driven a golf cart," Ginny said.

"Oh, it's easy. I'll show you how." And with that Betty eased herself into the driver's seat, waited for their clubs to be loaded, and then took off driving in circles while waiting for the others.

"Slow down," Ginny cried, hanging on to the windshield. "You'll hit something."

"Don't you worry, it's like riding a bike. You never forget." With that Betty headed for the first tee. "We'll go ahead of you, since we'll be a little faster," she called to Frank over her shoulder.

Ginny sent her husband a desperate look as if she had just been kidnapped.

Stopped at the women's tee box, Ginny confessed she didn't really want to drive the ball.

"Even better!" Betty said gaily, and they soared down the slight incline and headed for the green. "Isn't this wonderful?"

Ginny was less enthused, as the bumping over the rough ground was making her stomach hurt.

Betty pulled up alongside the green and came to a stop. Ginny threw her ball out and made a serious attempt to sink her putt. It took four strokes but she got it in. "Your turn," she said to Betty.

"Oh, I don't think I'll play. All that getting in and out of the cart will wear me out. I'll just drive."

Ginny got back into the cart and studied her friend.

"Did you bring us all out here just so could drive a cart?"

"Why not? I really miss driving."

"But it was over $250!"

"I can't take it with me. Aren't you having fun? Here, you take a turn behind the wheel."

They switched seats, and Ginny grudgingly admitted to herself that, while putting on the green was enjoyable, driving the cart in the wide open spaces on a beautiful day was, in fact, VERY fun. She drove for a few holes, then let Betty do the rest of the driving. In all, they probably covered the course three times because Betty kept circling back to see how the others were doing.

"You're going to get thrown off the course," Paul mentioned on one of their drive-bys.

"I'm dying. So what?" Betty replied cheerily and she zoomed around them and headed off again. "Besides, no one can see us back here. I picked a non-busy time."

Ginny decided she wouldn't mention the outing to Tess or Lindsay. It would be hard to explain the simple joy of acting like a kid again.

Chapter Thirty-One

The week after Labor Day, Betty requested a drive toward Steven's Pass to see the turning leaves.

"It's too early for the leaves to be turning," Paul said.

"I know, but I would like to get out in nature one last time."

So the crew decided to take a leisurely drive, and packed a picnic lunch. They stopped here and there to admire the view or an object of interest, and ate their sandwiches at a campground picnic table beside the Skykomish River. On the way home, they passed an open field with several horses, including a young colt.

"Stop, could you please, Paul? I want to look at those horses."

Paul slowed the van down so they could observe the idyllic scene.

"No," Betty said firmly. "Stop. I want to get out and really see them."

Paul sighed. He hadn't minded stopping at the Wayside Chapel, with its "Pause...Rest...Worship" sign beckoning travelers to enjoy a peaceful moment. He had snapped some nice pictures of the group in the tiny house of worship, complete with four small pews and a pulpit. He had even stood at the pulpit as if ready to deliver a sermon to his tiny congregation. It was a nice moment.

But now he was ready to be home before the evening traffic started in earnest, and stopping to look at horses wasn't on his list. Besides, there wasn't much room to pull off the road before getting into the high grass. He glanced in the rear view mirror and saw Betty looking brightly at him from her perch in the middle back seat of the van. With a sigh, he pulled over, opened the doors, and Joan hopped out then turned to help Betty. Ginny came from the other side and

160

joined their friend at the wooden fence, as she called to the horses with an odd whistle and cooing sound.

Frank was also ready to be home. "You probably shouldn't bother them," he said, easing himself out of the van and looking for a posted No Trespassing sign.

"Don't be ridiculous. My father had a farm, and people were always welcome to stop and see the horses," Betty admonished him. She made another unsuccessful attempt to call the mare and foal over, pulling some long grass and waving it between the horizontal fence slats of the enclosure.

"Hmm." Betty was disappointed. Her eye caught a small shed a short way up the farmer's drive. "I need to pee, desperately," she told the group. "I'm just going to go up behind that shack. I'll be right back."

"I'll go with you," Joan said.

"Don't be silly. Lord willing, I can still pee by myself." And with that she was off.

The foursome watched, remarking on her new-found strength since beginning three sessions a week of physical therapy. Holistic or wholistic, whatever it was had worked wonders so far. They still carried the portable oxygen when they were out, but Betty hadn't needed oxygen during the day for several weeks.

While they waited, a county sheriff's car approached, and the four watched as the officer pulled in behind the van and got out of his car. Paul had a sinking feeling and automatically felt to be sure his wallet with his driver's license was in his pocket.

"Any trouble, folks?" the middle-aged officer asked congenially.

"No. Just stopped to look at the horses for a moment," Paul answered. "Our friend—" he glanced back at the shack and then caught movement in the field. There was Betty, marching across the field toward the mare, still waving the grass.

The officer had also now caught sight of the red-jacketed, petite woman making her way through the rough ground. "She's with you?" he asked.

Ginny was aghast. "Betty!" she cried sharply. "Get out of there."

"This farmer is pretty mellow, but most don't appreciate strangers in their fields," the officer said while keeping his eyes on the red jacket.

"Of course not," Joan said. "She slipped off and must have climbed between the rails. We thought she was making a pit stop behind the shack."

"Most farmers aren't too crazy about that, either," the officer added.

"I'll get her," Frank said, then calling, "Stay there, Betty, I'm coming," as he squeezed between the split wood fence rails.

By this time Betty had closed the distance to the mare, and was very softly cooing her way within reach. To the surprise of all, the mare took several steps toward her and allowed her long black nose to be rubbed. The colt also came up alongside for some stroking.

"Who knew we had a damn horse whisperer in the house?" Paul said under his breath.

Ginny tried to be mad, but it was such a beautiful moment she nudged Joan to take a picture on her phone for Tess.

The approach of Frank and the deputy startled the mare and she and the colt skittered away. Betty had turned and started walking back to them when suddenly she went down with a startled, "Oh, no," tripping on the rough ground and unfortunately landing in horse dung.

The deputy reached her first followed quickly by Frank, whose attempts to step carefully had slowed him down.

"I didn't mean to be a bother," Betty said to the officer. "I'm on my deathbed, you see." She managed a fairly convincing cough to drive home the point.

"I think at this moment you're in the middle of a field that doesn't belong to you," the officer extended his hand to her clean one, hauling her to her feet.

"I just wanted to touch a horse one last time. Please don't be angry with my friends."

"No harm done."

Frank had finally reached Betty at this point. Seeing that she was intact, each gentleman took an elbow, steadying her on the way back, despite her protestations.

"They were lovely," Betty said to the others, carefully climbing through the fence. "It reminds me so of my father's farm." She had dung on her shoes, one hand, up the back of her pants and on her jacket. "Well worth the inconvenience."

"Oh, Betty. Honestly!" Paul said with some impatience, thinking of the van's seats.

"Oh, dear," Joan added, taking a few more pictures of their unremorseful patient and realizing the extent of the problem. "I haven't kept trash bags and towels in the car since the boys quit playing soccer in their teens. I don't know how we'll get you home."

"We could strap her to the roof," Paul said, only half joking.

"I can help," the deputy said, going back to his patrol unit and opening the trunk. He pulled several black plastic trash bags out and a roll of paper towels and offered them to Joan. "Here."

"Yes, just the thing. Thank you, officer. We can't thank you enough."

Wrapping Betty in the plastic and removing her shoes, she was sandwiched between the women in the back seat. It required lowering all four windows halfway down to put up with the stench, but by the time they pulled into the driveway, everyone but Paul was laughing.

The manure stained clothing went right into the trash. With the afternoon's exertion and the effort to get up the stairs to the shower,

Ginny and Joan had no trouble tucking a pliant Betty into bed and getting the oxygen on her.

A little later Frank arrived with a dinner tray. "Paul says you're grounded, by the way," he said, placing Ginny's homemade chicken soup and salad before the reclining Betty.

"No harm, no foul."

"Only because the deputy had a sense of humor and a good supply of evidence bags. It could have been a real mess getting you home."

"Oh, I could have stripped down to my underwear and come home like that." Betty took a dribbling bite of hot noodles. "Umm, this is good. But needs some salt."

"And wouldn't you in your underwear have made an interesting sight if we'd gotten pulled over? You half-naked in the back seat!"

"You all worry too much. Wait till you're on *your* deathbed, your tune will change."

"And that's another thing. I'm not sure that deathbed thing is going to work much longer, since you're out and about dancing through horse fields and doing wheelies on the golf course."

"You're right," Betty flashed him her megawatt smile. "I'll save it for emergencies."

In bed that night, Betty closed her eyes and could see the wise and gentle eyes of the mare before her, remembering the feel of the rough coat under her fingertips and the soft nudging of the colt's nose as he took the grass from her hand.

She slept soundly all night and didn't wake up coughing one time.

Chapter Thirty-Two

"It's Tess," Frank handed Betty the house phone after finally finding her sitting on the patio in the rain, huddled under her umbrella and blanket. "What are you doing out here, anyway? It's chilly. And you need to have that scarf I bought you around your face. This cold air isn't good for you."

"I needed some fresh air," Betty put the phone up to her ear. "Hello, honey. I'm so sorry, I left my phone beside the bed."

"That's okay. You're sitting outside? In this weather? Do you think that's good for you?"

"I don't care what the doctor says, I think the cool air helps my lungs. Now what can I do for you?"

Tess swallowed the words she really wanted to say about her mother's attitude regarding sound medical advice, and continued with the reason for her call. "Claire has a choir concert tonight at school. She has a solo. I wondered if you'd like to come?"

Betty considered for a moment. It had been some time since Tess had asked her to go somewhere. "I'd love to. What time?"

"I need to drop her at school at 6:30. I'll pick you up at 7, the concert starts at 7:30."

"Okay, I'll be ready."

When Tess arrived, Betty was waiting in the living room, a new heavy winter coat draped over the chair, her handbag packed with cough drops, and the handicapped parking placard nearby.

"How about the oxygen?" Tess said. "Shouldn't we take it along?"

"Oh, I don't need it. We won't be gone that long. I'm good today."

Tess and Frank helped Betty into the car, and Tess headed for the school.

"Thank you for inviting me," Betty said awkwardly, fiddling with her seatbelt.

"I'm sorry I haven't been able to take you out more often," Tess said, more defensively than she meant. "It's been busy at work. Holidays just around the corner."

"I know, honey. Believe me, I'm perfectly content. Ginny and Frank, Joan and Paul—they've been wonderful to me. It's working out very well."

Tess hadn't brought up anything about the horse farm adventure, waiting to see if her mother's version eventually matched the pictures she'd received from Joan. As she suspected, Betty's report left out a few details: traipsing through the field, slipping in the dung, and the sheriff and his evidence bags coming to the rescue. "Saw some horses on our drive the other day," was all her mother had said. "Reminded me of my father's horse farm when I was little."

At the high school, Tess settled her mom into an auditorium seat in the back row on the aisle, and they both perused the program bulletin. Betty noted with some concern that Claire's piece didn't come until near the end. For some reason, she had assumed the freshman's solo would be in the first half of the program.

The lights dimmed and the tenth grade chorale took the stage. Betty viewed the auditorium, completely filled with parents and students. The four pieces were lively and well-sung. Next up was a boys' chorus. Betty's attention began to wander by the second selection, and her legs were getting antsy. She tried to do some deep breathing, but now her chest felt as if it might explode, and she had to fight her panicky feelings. She'd had this odd claustrophobia for years now, any time she was in a large crowd without an easy exit. Half-way through the next group, an acapella triple trio, she leaned over to Tess.

"I have to leave. I'll wait for you in the lobby." She pulled herself up and took a step into the aisle.

"Mom! At least wait until the piece is over!" Tess whispered loudly. But Betty was already to the heavy auditorium door. Tess gathered their belongings and followed her, pushing the door for her mother who suddenly looked very petite and frail.

Betty took two steps into the lobby and then stopped to catch her breath. She should have brought the oxygen, she realized, but she hated it so. She hated to wear it, she hated what it represented, she hated being labeled as old and ill.

"Mom, wait."

"I'm so sorry, Tess. Could you run me home? You'll still have time to get back before Claire's solo."

Tess looked at the time with resignation. She wouldn't make it back.

"Could you wait here in the lobby?"

"I don't think so," Betty gasped. "I underestimated the effort it took to walk in here. Even with the ramp, it was a climb."

Tess tried not to think of her mother tromping through the farmer's field just last week. She helped her mother into her coat, and resolutely took her elbow as they made their way to the car. Betty was taking odd little breaths that Tess hadn't heard before, and once in the car finally let loose with some wracking coughs. Tess offered her mother a sip from her water bottle, but Betty just shook her head.

Tess called ahead and asked if someone could meet her mother at the car, hoping for a quick turn around on the slim chance she could make it back to hear her daughter sing.

"Tell Claire it was a lovely concert," Betty said between wheezes as she left the car.

"Will do, Mom."

167

Tears slid down Tess's face as she drove back to the school, as familiar feelings of guilt, disappointment, and anger overwhelmed her. It had always been this way, plans attempted that somehow didn't work out and had to be reconstructed, either because of her father's drinking or some inexplicable change in her mother's demeanor once they arrived at the destination. A few years of counseling had made the patterns more clear, but not the reasons for them. Her mother was an extrovert in so many ways, but once she was done, she was done.

Ginny helped Betty undress and get into bed.

"What happened?" she asked kindly, getting the oxygen turned on. "You didn't stay for Claire's solo?"

Betty shook her head, and tears slid down her cheeks.

"For heaven's sake, Betty! What's wrong?" Ginny pulled the covers up tenderly. "I don't understand."

"I couldn't stay," Betty said morosely. "I had to get out of there."

"But why? You've had such a good day today."

There was a long pause before Betty confessed quietly, "I was afraid I'd start to cough during her solo. I could feel it coming. I should have taken the oxygen, I'm such a vain old fool. Now I ruined it for Tess."

Ginny sat on the side her friend's bed and patted her softly. "Tess understands. At least you tried. That counts for something."

Betty sighed. "I don't know. Zero plus zero is still zero."

Tess called Lindsay as soon as she got home that evening. She had arrived at the auditorium to hear the last notes of Claire's performance. Fuming, she let loose a tirade while Lindsay did her best to listen empathetically without offering advice.

"And where does it say that just because I'm the girl, I'm the one who has to take care of her?" Tess continued angrily. "My brothers and their families haven't been to visit in a year. You'd think one of them could fly in for a weekend. They barely even call." Having nearly

168

raised her younger brothers, Tess did not take kindly to the distance they had put between themselves and their parents as soon as they went to college and got jobs out-of-state, and then married and settled far away.

"I'm sorry, Tess. I'm sorry for all of it, but especially that you had to miss her solo."

"Oh, it's all right," Tess's voice bore the familiar sound of her resignation. "I've heard her practice that piece a hundred times. At least I made it for the applause."

Suddenly Lindsay could hear full-scale weeping on the line.

"Mom looked so frail," Tess finally managed to get out. "She just looked so frail."

Chapter Thirty-Three

Having gone to bed early the night before with a headache, Ginny was the first one awake and descending the stairs in the November morning darkness.

A frightened "Oh!" escaped her as she flicked on the living room light and a dark shape on the couch startled upright, rolled off the sofa, and released a loud expletive when hitting the floor. Ginny grabbed an umbrella from its place by the front door and held it protectively.

"Who are you?" Ginny demanded loudly, as footsteps above indicated Frank had been alerted and was on his way.

"I'm Scott, a friend of Betty's." The shape labored to its feet, shedding the thin blanket he was wrapped in and now appearing to be a less threatening elderly man, struggling to get glasses on the bridge of his nose. "I'm so sorry I frightened you. I realized last night that I shouldn't drive home, so I slept on your couch. Everyone had gone to bed, there was no one to ask. Betty said it would be all right."

Ginny relaxed her defensive stance as Frank came down the stairs behind her. "Oh," he said. "It's you."

"What's going on?" Now Joan was behind Frank on the stairs. "Oh," she noticed the man by the couch. "Hello, Scott. Did you decide to spend the night?"

"Yes, one beer too many, I think. And the rainy night. Betty said it would be all right if I stayed, but I'm sorry I've caused a ruckus this morning." He straightened his clothing. "Do you mind if I use the rest room before I get on my way?"

"Of course not," Joan said. "You're welcome to stay for breakfast, if you like."

Once he was out of earshot, Ginny turned to the others. "Who on earth?"

"An old friend of Betty's. He stopped by last night after you'd gone to bed. She asked for a couple of beers and they ordered a pizza. That's all I know. Her door was closed when I went upstairs." Joan made her way to the kitchen. "I'll start the coffee."

"I think I'd better check on Betty," Ginny said, going down the hall quietly. She opened the door and observed Betty sound asleep, her oxygen on, and a group of six beer bottles and the empty pizza box on Frank's desk.

Their overnight guest was gone by the time Ginny returned to the kitchen.

"Why did you give them all that beer?" she asked her husband accusingly. "They went through a six-pack!"

Frank shrugged. "Her friend arrived, she asked if we had any beer, and I gave it to them. She's never asked for alcohol before."

"I'm calling Tess." Ginny marched to the living room in a huff and punched in the familiar number.

"Hey," Tess picked up quickly. Calls before eight a.m. were rarely good news. "Everything okay?"

"Yes, I think so, but I wanted to check. Your mother had a male friend over last night. They drank a six pack of beer and ordered a pizza. Then I found him asleep on the couch when I came downstairs this morning. He nearly scared me to death! His name is Scott."

"Oh, Scott," Tess relaxed at the household name, "One of my father's business partners. They're old friends. His wife died years ago. I'm sorry he scared you. He's a nice guy."

"Do you think it's okay for your mom to be drinking beer? They went through a six-pack."

"She's never drunk much beer. Is she okay this morning?"

"She's not up yet. But I checked, and she's breathing."

"All right, I'll call her later."

Ginny arrived at the dining room table, still flustered and desperately hoping her headache from the night before wouldn't be triggered by her pounding heart. "All the years we worried about our kids not driving drunk," she settled down in her chair and flipped the newspaper open. "Now we have to start over with Betty's friends?"

"It's probably a one-time thing," Frank consoled her. "She's on her deathbed, you know. Anyway, he seemed like an okay fellow."

Paul joined them and they finished their morning routines, with Ginny checking on Betty every so often and finally rousing her at eleven to take her medicines.

"Oh," Betty moaned, her hand on her head. "Could you get me an aspirin? My head is splitting."

"Are you allowed to mix aspirin with these meds?"

"What's the worst it can do, kill me?"

"Fine." Ginny brought back a bottle of pills and a fresh glass of water. "What on earth was going on after I went to bed? Your friend nearly gave me a heart attack this morning. I didn't know anyone else was in the house."

"Oh, sorry," Betty murmured, swallowing two aspirin and then closing her eyes again. "We had a lovely evening. He brought his computer and we watched a movie, had beer and pizza. Except for the hospital bed and a bad headache this morning, it was a delightful time."

"What did you watch?"

"That Steve Martin and John Candy movie, "Trains, Planes and Automobiles." It's so funny, we laughed and laughed. I love both of those actors."

"Hmm." Ginny considered. "Well, laughter IS good for you, I know that much. I guess I won't bar him from the door. But maybe next time I could leave him a pillow and a heavier blanket. I'm thankful he didn't drive home, but he was probably freezing on the couch."

"He's extra careful at night, says his eyes bother him. I hadn't seen him since before I moved into that assisted living place. He used to come over once a month or so before that. We'd have dinner and watch a movie. I miss that."

Ginny observed the patient, once again surprised at Betty's ability to wrestle the best out of her situation. "I love Steve Martin and John Candy, too. Maybe we could have a marathon movie series and watch all their old movies. Would you like that?" Ginny's earlier grumpiness was giving way to her more usual compassion.

"Sure. Now, do you mind turning off the light and going away? I'm going back to sleep. And here, take my phone. I'm assuming Tess will be calling at some point. Tell her I'm fine." With that Betty closed her eyes.

Summarily dismissed, Ginny took the phone and turned off the light.

At lunch, Ginny tried to put her uncomfortable feelings into words. "What is our purpose? Are we protecting her from herself? And to what end?"

"People's personalities don't change just because they're dying," Paul said. "In fact, I think certain elements become even more exaggerated. Certainly some people take risks they never would otherwise. They have nothing to lose."

Ginny sighed. "I know this was my idea. I didn't think she'd be quite so...so..."

"High maintenance?" Joan finished.

"Long lived?" Frank suggested.

"Sort of. She seemed so ill in the nursing home. I thought she was going gently into the good night."

"Apparently no one told her that," Paul quipped. "You should be proud of the care you and Joan have provided. You've made her better. And Frank, by insisting she quit smoking, you've vastly improved her quality of life."

"I guess," Ginny sighed. "But what's next?"

"I wouldn't worry about it," Paul said. "The path is uncertain, and it's not as easy to get out of this world as you might think. As long as she's feeling positive, she can probably keep herself going a little longer than anyone expected. I've seen the mind-body connection do amazing things. Let her be happy."

"Fine," Ginny retorted. "You said it. But I will remind you that almost having your van's seats covered in horse manure represented a happy moment for her and a less so one for you."

"Happy and *grounded*," Paul clarified. "Or we start using your Jeep instead of the van."

On Friday night of that week, Ginny asked Betty if she'd like to join them for a movie night. They'd rented Steve Martin's "All of Me" and John Candy's "Uncle Buck" as the first in their favorite comedians series. Settled on the couch and in comfortable chairs, the group went through a taco dinner, then devoured Ginny's fresh chocolate chip cookies and popcorn, finally topping the evening off with hot chocolate as the movies played.

In bed, Ginny patted Frank's chest happily. "I haven't laughed that much in ages," she said. "It felt good."

"I like seeing Betty happy. I thought your idea to bring her here was crazy originally," Frank squeezed Ginny a little tighter. "But I like making a difference for her, and for Tess. And the kids. It feels good."

Ginny rolled over and pondered the many odd turns their life with Betty had taken, while the soundtrack from "All of Me" played in her head.

Chapter Thirty-Four

Betty and her therapist were taking a short walk along the popular walking and bike path, the Burke-Gilman Trail, near the house, when Betty noticed the smallest rustle under a bush just off the path.

"What is that?" she pointed with her walking stick.

A whimpering sound came from beneath the leaves and fallen boughs. Bonnie, the physical therapist, delicately stepped down the slight incline, trying to keep her sturdy work shoes free of the muck. She pulled off the debris.

"It's a dog!"

Sad sunken eyes in a black and white, pathetically thin little body looked at her listlessly. She scooped the dog up gently and carried the bundle back to Betty.

"It's just a puppy," Betty said. "Look at its leg!"

"Something must have got to it," Bonnie tried to cradle the dog while supporting the injured limb.

"I'm calling Frank," Betty said impulsively. "He can pick us up and we'll go straight to that vet by the shopping center."

Frank was paying the November bills. He had gotten used to Betty's interruptions, but a dog emergency was a new one. He understood her kind heart, and her description of the dog's desperate condition supported a sense of urgency, so he yelled to Ginny, found a box, grabbed some old towels, and headed for the Jeep.

"We'll meet you there!" Joan called after them, learning the details as Ginny and Frank went out the door.

"I don't think we need five of us," Frank started to say, but then realized it was hopeless. Any medical emergency, and Joan would be front and center in the response.

Betty and her therapist had made their way back to the nearest street access to the trail, where they waited for rescue.

"What took so long?" Betty asked sharply, as Bonnie laid the pup in the box and covered her with a towel. "Look at this poor thing."

"Get in the car and we'll be on our way. Thank you, Bonnie. You've got other clients to see this morning?"

"Yes," she turned to Betty, "but call me later and let me know what happens, okay?"

"Of course, of course," Betty said impatiently. "Come on, let's get going."

With the box on the back seat beside her, Betty wiped the mud from the pup's face with one edge of the towel. The pup made a feeble effort to lick her hand.

"Poor baby. Who would do such a thing, leave you out there in such condition?"

The vet tech put them in the extra exam room, reserved for emergencies and not particularly spacious.

"Do you have a heat lamp?" Joan asked, sliding the miserable and shivering heap of fur onto the exam table.

"Shouldn't we wait for the doctor?" Ginny inquired anxiously.

"She's in pretty bad shape," Joan replied, her hand on its chest, counting respirations. "But I can feel a steady little heart beat in there."

At her touch, the white, paint-tipped tail gave a small flick.

"Come on, baby, you'll be okay," Joan felt the injured limb. "I don't think it's broken. But something punctured the skin for sure. Maybe another dog, or a coyote."

At this point, the veterinarian arrived, accompanied by the tech again.

"Hello—," she glanced in surprise around the small room packed with five adults,

"— everyone. So, a puppy in distress?" The emaciated little head stayed flat on the table while the doctor checked every part.

"All right. We'll start an IV and do fluids, antibiotics, and pain meds. Clean up this wound and get an x-ray of the leg. I'd say she's about 8 weeks old. She's pretty small, might have been the runt. Obviously malnourished. Some fluids and pain meds will make a big difference. We'll see what's going on with her. If she's stable, you can pick her up tomorrow."

"We're not—" Frank started to say.

"Thank you so much doctor," Betty interrupted him. "Whatever you need to do to make her comfortable, cost is not an issue. I'm covering it." Betty spoke with her usual finality, and the others were not invited to weigh in.

The next afternoon, having brought the slightly more alert puppy home, a serious conversation ensued in Betty's room, where Ginny, Frank, and the great rescuer Betty peered into the box on the floor.

"I want to keep her," Betty announced. "I found her, I want to keep her."

Frank and Ginny's faces indicated concern.

"It wouldn't be for long. I've checked with Tess. She said she'd take her when I—" Betty paused dramatically, "—pass."

"Don't take this the wrong way," Frank looked at his friend kindly. "But you're about four months overdue for that event at this point."

"It's hardly my fault that my demise has been postponed," Betty stiffened. "It's quite an honor to be thrown out of hospice. You've taken such good care of me. I'd think you'd be pleased."

"Of course we're pleased," Ginny soothed her friend. "And you weren't thrown out of hospice. But, it's just, you know, sometimes people like to decide about having a pet ahead of time, rather than having one thrust upon them."

"No one's thrusting anything on anyone. I'll take care of her, I promise."

"That's what every ten-year-old says who drags home a lost animal," Frank remarked dryly.

"So I'm going backwards in life. Sue me. Think of it as a therapy dog. A companion dog."

"The four of us aren't enough?" Ginny sank to the floor cross-legged beside the box.

"Now you can go out in the evening and not worry about me being alone."

Ginny gently stroked the black and white fur, being careful to avoid the bandaged leg. The little tongue found her hand. The eyes had definitely brightened up.

"I suppose she can stay until her owners find her. At least the back yard is already fenced. But you'll have to train her, Betty…take her in and out all the time. It's like having a baby. I'm afraid you'll get attached to her, and then it will be so hard if you have to give her up."

"And what about our travels plans?" Frank was still skeptical.

"I have that all worked out," Betty said. "Tess offered to keep her. Her kids would love to have a dog, it's just never worked out before. Plus the puppy could probably ride along in the motor home, anyway."

"Absolutely not," said Frank. "No kids, no dogs."

That evening Lindsay reported to Tess, "They have lost their minds. They've all gone crazy over this dog. Even Mo's parents, and they never wanted any pets at all while the boys were growing up. It's nuts."

"I'm really sorry, this is all my mom's fault. We never had a dog growing up, either. I can't imagine what has made her so anxious to take one on. Now, of all times."

"And you're really okay with taking it…after?"

"The boys have been requesting a dog for years. I don't mind. And the owner might still show up, anyway. Someone must be looking for it."

"I hope so." Lindsay was mostly hoping that she could keep Alex from falling in love with the puppy and then wanting one of his own, a situation she had managed to dodge with extreme effort with his older sisters.

The little black and white lab mix's addition to the household had the happy and unintended consequence of bringing all the grandchildren over more often, including Betty's grandsons and granddaughter. Joan and Ginny made a quick trip to the pet store, arriving home with a medium-sized crate for Betty's room, food, a second bed pad for the kitchen, and a myriad of puppy chew toys. After several weeks, none of them could imagine how they lived without the perky and pesky little dog in their lives. Betty was true to her word, getting the pup trained to go outside in pretty short order, even with the shortened days and wet, windy weather. Someone went with her three times a day when she walked the dog up and down in front of their house, her own footsteps continuing to improve remarkably despite her doctor's original warning of "short-term" reprieve.

As Ginny worked at her computer one morning in mid-November, an unknown name popped up in her inbox, with "lost dog" in the re: line. An anxious shudder went through her as she opened the message: "Saw your flyer at trail. Our dog's lab/border collie puppies escaped from the yard two miles from the trail in October. Six of the seven recovered. We stopped looking after two weeks for the last one. Her name is Ernestine." And then a phone number. Ginny reread the note several times. She and Frank had contacted several nearby vet's offices, and still had flyers up along the trail. Now here it was weeks later.

She wasn't giving the dog back, that's all there was to it. She closed her eyes, said a quick apology to God for her selfishness, and pressed the delete key. "And her name is Luna, by the way," she said to the deleting message.

Frank was in the garage, working on an indestructible doll house he was building for Mara and Francie for Christmas, when an unfamiliar number came up with a text on his phone: "Saw your Found notice on the trail. Could be one of our puppies that wandered away."

"Could be," Frank muttered to himself, "but I doubt it." He erased the text without another thought. Later, he saw Ginny pass by the open garage door.

"Where are you going?" he asked.

"To walk the trail a little bit. I need to stretch my legs. And I think it's time to take down those 'Found' notices, don't you?"

"Yup. Hold on, I'll come with you." He put down the drill and grabbed his jacket. "You go south, I'll go north."

Chapter Thirty-Five

A week before Thanksgiving, Ginny and Joan sat at the dining room table, pen and paper poised, to begin planning for the mighty feast.

"Let's start with how many we'll have this year," Joan suggested. "For our side, it will just be Lindsay and Mo and the three kids. Joseph and Tristan are going to come out for New Year's."

"Okay. For us, let's see. Pam is coming from D.C., but not until December 27. So that leaves Sophie and her girls, possibly Sophie's new boyfriend; Lindsay and all, you've already got them; Robert, Jill, Mara and Francie."

"Good. Then Betty. What about Tess?"

"I'm sure she'll come. Not sure about her kids, though. Seems to me this year they spend Thanksgiving with their father."

"So that makes somewhere between 16 and 21. That's about the same as past years."

"Why on earth don't we keep our plans in a folder so we don't have to start from square one each year?" Ginny sighed, knowing that dietary preferences were next to be considered.

"You've always done most of the work, Ginny. I've just breezed in here at the last minute with my salad and store-bought pumpkin pies in hand. But this year, I can really be of some help, if you'll let me."

"Of course. You know your way around the kitchen now, so have at it."

They worked on the menu next. Sophie had mentioned to her mother that her teens were now completely abstaining from meat, and they would prepare a meatless Tofurkey and bring it with them. Along with some vegan gravy. Betty and Joan worked their way through the rest of the meal.

"All right, then," Joan looked at her neatly printed list. "Twenty-pound turkey, bought gravy, mashed potatoes, sweet potatoes, green bean casserole, stuffing, green salad, rolls, apple pies, blueberry pies, and pumpkin pies; vegetable plate and cheese and crackers for appetizers. Chocolate chip cookies for the non-pie eaters. Ice cream for the pie. Coffee. Oh, and wine and beer."

"We will definitely be needing the wine," Ginny mumbled, although nearly everyone being together at Thanksgiving did delight her. She had even mastered having the meal all done at the same time, although hot on the last plate served was still a challenge. "Let's forego trying to seat everyone at the table, and serve buffet off the kitchen counters and stove top. We'll let people eat wherever they like. What do you think about that?"

"Sounds good to me."

The weather turned cold the weekend before Thanksgiving, with uncertain forecasts predicting snow and wind for various times and locations around Puget Sound through the holiday. Ginny decided to get her shopping done early, which was a good thing as by Sunday, snow, cold and slippery streets were causing the usual havoc on Seattle's hills.

Thanksgiving Day began with a few snow flurries, but gradually warmed up. The house was filled with the aroma of the roasting bird, while the smells from the pie baking extravaganza of the night before still lingered.

Betty, wanting to be of help, had ordered a gargantuan floral arrangement for the centerpiece, which, despite the weather, was delivered on time. Ginny looked at the three-foot-long box and could not imagine where she was going to put the lavish array of red and orange birds of paradise, which happened to be her personal favorite.

182

The troops began arriving around 2:00 for a dinner at 5:00. Tess's children accompanied their mother, their father being sensitive to the possibility that this could be Betty's last Thanksgiving, and willing to trade weekends. Tess was thankful, although not so indebted as to invite him and his new girlfriend to join them. She and her ex had managed to remain friends through the six years since the divorce, and they were good parents together. But, though she would admit it to no one but Lindsay, the addition of the girlfriend into the equation had thrown off the family balance, and Tess had not quite learned how to deal with it.

Betty joined all the guests for dinner, but then returned to her room when a coughing fit interrupted her meal. Tess went back and forth from the den to the table, checking on her mother. The plates were scraped and stacked in the kitchen, while everyone rested and someone put on the annual showing of the original *How the Grinch Stole Christmas*. After dessert, Robert and Jill gathered Mara and little Francie and prepared to leave.

An odd, hoarse coughing suddenly emanated from the kitchen, as Alex yelled in a frightened voice for his grandmother, "Noni! Help! Luna's choking! She got into the garbage!"

The three-month-old pup, left to her own devices after Betty withdrew to her room, had been surreptitiously snacking on whatever she could reach in the garbage, which had accidentally been left on the floor instead of its usual spot high up on a chair. When Ginny came through the door, the dog's terrified look and gasping cough had Alex in a near panic. Joan, right behind her friend, instructed Ginny to hold the dog firmly. Quickly catching the pup's mouth in her hands, she pushed Luna's long tongue out of the way, and peered in to find the obstruction.

"I can't see anything," Joan said. "Let's get her head down."

Ginny picked up the struggling dog, holding her head low and butt higher, and followed Joan's directions to shake her a bit. Joan explored the dog's mouth again with her fingers without success.

"Is there a dog Heimlich?" Ginny asked, hearing Betty coming down the hall after being summoned by her grandsons.

"I don't know. I'll try." Joan estimated the probable point below the dog's rib cage and gave a fairly sharp push. Nothing happened the first time, but after repositioning the upside-down Luna, trying to get a straight shot out for the offending object, another sharp rap earned a piece of turkey thigh bone being propelled onto the floor.

Ginny collapsed, holding the still shaking pup, just as Betty came through the door with Tess and the others behind her.

"What happened?" Betty asked in dismay. "What's wrong?"

"Choked on a turkey bone. She's okay," Joan patted Luna's head.

"I should have taken her to the room with me," Betty cried. "Oh, Luna, you poor puppy!" Betty bent to envelop the dog in her arms and burst into tears.

"She's okay, Betty," Joan comforted her. "I think she'll be okay. Let's see if she'll take a drink."

But Betty's emotions had overwhelmed her, and with wracking sobs she retreated unsteadily to her room.

Tess watched her mom from the doorway, transfixed by her mother's emotional display. Lindsay came up behind her friend.

"I don't think I've ever seen my mother cry before, even when Dad died," Tess said to Lindsay curiously. "She never cried over us, I know that." Tears welled up in her eyes, and soon were streaming down her face. "She cares more about that damn dog than she ever did us. No wonder my brothers have no desire to be here. "

Ginny went to her almost-daughter and folded her into a hug, whispering into her ear. The remarks made Tess cry even harder.

Frank, coming in the back door after throwing some salt on the remaining icy patches on the sidewalks, heard Betty sobbing and coughing in her room, and then entered the kitchen where Tess was having a moment on his wife's shoulder and his daughter looked like she was near tears herself.

"Why is everyone crying?" he asked.

"Luna choked on a bone. It was rather alarming," Joan told him. "Scared everyone."

Even though the degree of emotional response in the kitchen didn't seem to match the event, Frank knew better than to question anyone further at the moment. He continued to the front door where Robert and Jill were again trying to say their good-byes, and held the little girls' hands so they wouldn't slip as they made their way to the car.

In bed that night, Ginny tried to explain the dynamics of the evening's melt-down to her husband. "It's so hard on Tess, watching her mother go through this. Their relationship has always been rocky. I'm not sure why Betty was such a distant type of mother, but there's no doubt that she was. Tess practically raised her brothers herself. Her parents were like two bright stars circling each other, and there wasn't much room for the kids. And now it's all fallen on Tess's shoulders. I wish those boys would get out here and help her a little."

They were quiet with each other, Frank's arm behind Ginny's head. He hugged her tighter.

"You know you can't fix everything, honey, as much as you want to."

"I know," Ginny sighed, as her mind played over various improbable ideas. "But I doubt that will keep me from trying."

Chapter Thirty-Six

The December days were short, with the sun making its low arc across the sky and bringing gray daylight for less than nine hours a day.

Betty had joined the others for lunch, her fingers drumming impatiently on the table after she finished her small turkey sandwich, the dog curled at her feet waiting for a morsel.

"What is it?" Joan finally asked her noisy friend.

"I would like to see the ocean one more time before I die," Betty said abruptly.

"It's December," Paul stated the obvious. "The weather's terrible on the coast right now."

"How bad can it be? I just want to see the waves and smell the salt water. Just one more time."

"Ocean Shores wouldn't be such a long trip," Ginny put in, drawing stares of disbelief from the others. "It's only three hours or so from Seattle. We could take the van and stay in a motel."

Frank studied his wife, the farmer, the never-want-to-leave-home, happily-stuck-in-the-mud person he married, suddenly suspicious of a conspiracy.

"I checked and Tess said she'd keep Luna," Betty added helpfully. "The kids will love having her."

"What's in this for you?" Frank asked his wife. "It's less than four weeks until Christmas. I can't ever remember you wanting to leave home in the month of December."

"Well," Ginny admitted, "when Betty mentioned it to me yesterday, I realized that the Olympic rain forest is right on the way.

186

Sort of. On the way back, we could spend one night at Lake Quinault Lodge, and poke around there a little bit. Might be fun."

"Fun," Frank pondered. "In the cold and pouring rain. In the *rain forest* in winter."

"Oh, it's the trees," Joan figured it out. "I'm sure there must be some Big Trees on Ginny's list in the Olympic National Forest. Probably *all* the trees there are gargantuan, considering how much rain they get."

"That's right," Ginny admitted. "I would like to go see some of the big trees there. There's Coastal Douglas Fir, and Western Red Cedar, and Sitka Spruce. I'm not sure exactly where the biggest ones are, but, like Joan said, even the smaller ones are probably big. You know what I mean." She smiled hopefully at her husband.

"I happened to check the weather," Betty said. "We've got a clear couple of days coming up. Or at least a little less rain. Three days, two nights, that's all we'd need."

"I'm in," Paul said. "I'll get the van ready. Somebody else can work on reservations and the route."

"I will," Ginny said happily. "No problem. Pack light, but warmly," she advised.

"And we're taking the oxygen," Paul warned.

"No problem," Betty agreed, thrilled to be on the move again.

Thus several days later, with the dog making her first overnight visit to Tess's house, the traveling quintet arrived at Ocean Shores around noon, finding one of the public parks along the Pacific shoreline.

"It still seems odd to me," Joan said, after reading up about the area, "that you are allowed to drive on the beach. Did you know part of it is technically a state highway?"

Paul was slowly driving through an empty parking lot. No sign of the sun through the thick cloud cover, and it felt too cold to get Betty out of the car.

"Couldn't we get closer to the waves?" Betty asked. "I want to feel the spray on my face."

"I don't think so, Betty. This is about it."

"Can't you go down the boat ramp a bit? The tide is way out."

"I don't want to get stuck in the sand."

"Don't go in the sand, just stay on the ramp. It must be concrete or wood or something. Look how far out it stretches."

Paul considered the gently sloping ramp, deciding that it couldn't possibly be a boat ramp since it was still a hundred yards to the water's edge. Perhaps it was simply the entrance ramp for the few cars and trucks he had noticed farther up the beach, most likely belonging to the fishermen dotting the shoreline.

He turned the van onto the ramp and proceeded carefully twenty yards or so toward the water.

"That's it," he said.

"Oh, please, a little further?" Betty asked.

"Nope. This is it. We'll put the windows down a bit, maybe some spray will pass through. You can sure hear the waves well enough from here."

"Oh, fine." Betty took the deepest breath she could manage. "I think the fresh salt air is good for my lungs."

"You should write a book," Frank told her. "*All the Things My Doctor Said Not to Do That I Did Anyway and Haven't Killed Me Yet.*"

"The title needs work, but that's not a bad idea," Betty replied. "Pass me a blanket, would you please?" She intended to enjoy the sights and sounds of the waves for as long as she possibly could, even if it was from the third seat of the van.

"I'm going to walk back and find some coffee," Frank said. "Anyone else want to come?"

"I will," said Paul. "I'll leave the keys in the ignition."

"I'll stay with car," said Joan.

"Me, too," said Ginny.

Each woman grabbed a blanket, as the car was cooling down with the windows cracked open, and settled into their seats after being sure Betty was warm enough.

The rhythm of the crashing waves seemed to put everything else out of Ginny's mind, and in a few moments she had nodded off. She woke with a start forty-five minutes later, looking through the front windshield and trying to discern what she was seeing. It was water, clearly water, and it was much too close. Moving on its own across the sand toward them, it was now within thirty yards of the car, when before it had seemed a football-field-length away.

"Joan," she shook her friend awake. "Joan, the tide's coming in. Quick, you've got to back the van up."

Joan woke, and, after a few disorienting seconds, realized the impending peril. She was sliding the van door open to hop in the front seat, when Paul and Frank arrived, breathless. Paul jumped behind the wheel, started the car, and slowly backed up the ramp, with Frank standing behind to guide him.

The car movement woke Betty. "Oh, are we leaving already?" she asked sorrowfully.

"Tide's coming in," Ginny told her. "It's move or swim."

Safely back in the parking lot, the travelers watched in wonder as more of the beach disappeared, each wave of shore break carrying the tide farther in.

Frank had finally caught his breath from the dash back to the car.

"Where were you guys?" Joan asked. "I thought you were just getting coffee."

"We lost track of time in one of the shops. There's an interesting historical display, and we got chatting with the shopkeeper. When we said we'd left you all parked on the beach, he told us it's a shallow beach with a fast incoming tide. We apparently missed the warning sign about that. Anyway, it's possible hauling tourists' cars out of the water and sand is one of the main sources of income around here. He was shouting the name of a tow truck operator as we ran out of the shop."

"This is certainly exciting," Betty piped up from the back. "But I am glad we didn't get stuck. I wouldn't want to be responsible for ruining the van...again."

They headed for their beach motel, which had a magnificent ocean view. Betty was too tired to go out to eat a late lunch, so they left her tucked in bed where she could watch the waves, with the TV remote in one hand, her cell phone in the other, a peanut butter and jelly sandwich and her book bag within reach, and the portable oxygen on. "I'll be fine," she said. "Go out and have a good time."

The foursome wandered through town, locating what looked like an interesting place to get dinner before eating lunch at a sandwich shop, then went back to check on Betty. She was peacefully sitting in bed, watching the waves, writing some letters. "The boys," she answered, to Ginny's questioning look. "Some things I should have told them a long time ago."

Ginny thought of Tess, the dutiful daughter, and her struggles through the years with her mother, especially after her father George's death. She hoped Betty was telling her sons to get themselves together and make an appearance in the near future.

That evening they played a little bridge and watched TV, enjoying their adjoining rooms. The women had decided Paul and Joan would take Betty in the extra bed in their room the first night, and Ginny and Frank would take her the second night at the Lake Quinault Lodge in Olympic National Park.

In the morning, Ginny was anxious to get going, and she peered out the window the entire drive to the park like a five-year-old on her way to Disneyland for the first time.

The stone lodge was stunning, just as it appeared in the advertisements. After a quick lunch and short naps, they left Betty to rest in the room and went out, despite the rain, to investigate the trails across from the lodge.

Ginny looked up, and up, and up, through the moss-draped branches. The trees were so tall she couldn't see their tops. She could watch individual rain drops as they fell to earth, clearly distinguishable against the lush green canopy above her. After twenty minutes of walking they came to a bench, and Ginny decided to sit and wait while the others wandered on.

She had brought a plastic bag for just this purpose, and, spreading it out so as to keep her pants dry, she perched on the wood bench and closed her eyes. Surprisingly, being among the giants didn't make her feel insignificant, although in size and age she certainly was. It was more a feeling of connectedness, of the overall goodness of things, of how slowly the cycle of life turned in this forest. Of calm, and peace.

Her reverie was broken by the others as they arrived, cold and wet. They tromped back to the lodge. After dinner, they brought Betty, sans her oxygen tank, to sit with them in front of the roaring fire in the great stone hearth.

"What a magnificent place, don't you think?" Ginny asked them all.

"I can't believe we never came here," Joan commented to Paul, who was dozing off in his chair, his meal resting comfortably.

Paul considered the unhurriedness of the day, the warmth of the crackling fire, the ease of the drive, the joy of being with these friends. "It's possible," he nodded toward Ginny, "that foreign travel is highly over-rated. You might be making a farmer out of me after all."

"I haven't stood in line at an airport in over a year," Joan agreed. "And I don't miss it one bit!"

But Betty's night was a restless one, even with her oxygen, so they got an early start in the morning, making only one stop at the World's Largest Sitka Spruce pull-out. Betty waited in the car while the others took the short hike to the old master, which rose impressively from its surroundings, its gnarly gray roots like a giant's fingers firmly grabbing the earth.

Frank took Ginny's picture in front of the trunk so she could add it to her collection, then two more of the impressive view upward. It was impossible to do the tree justice in one photo.

Arriving back at the car, they decided to investigate the World's Largest Western Red Cedar another visit, as, despite her protestations, they could tell Betty was beginning to wear out, and it seemed time to head home.

Chapter Thirty-Seven

The days were very short now, with the winter solstice only a week away.

"Paul?" Betty called from her bedroom. "Paul?"

"I'm coming," Paul replied from the kitchen, where he'd been rinsing the dinner dishes.

"What's up?" he poked his head in the den. Betty had been uncharacteristically somber the last few days, foregoing her daily walks, taking longer naps, the dog curled at the bottom of her bed. The four had discussed it and thought the cold and darkness of the days had gotten the better of their friend. It would be the end of January before daylight even approached ten hours.

"Come sit for a moment, will you?"

"Of course," Paul dried his hands on the dish towel he was carrying and moved the straight-backed desk chair to the bedside, noting that Luna had been chewing on the chair's leg again. "What can I do for you?" His silver hair neatly parted, his intense blue eyes observing her calmly, his manner warm and open; Betty could understand why he had been so successful in ministry and teaching. He exuded welcome and acceptance.

"I've been thinking a lot about it, and I'd like to take communion." Betty played with the edge of her blanket, sounding more shy than he had ever heard her before. "You could do that, right?"

"Of course. I don't have any wafers, but we could make do. But what's brought this on?"

"A lot of things. I didn't really expect to still be living by Christmas. Recently my breathing's gotten worse. I can feel my heart thwacking around all the time. Maybe one morning I'm not going to wake up. So it probably wouldn't hurt, you know, to touch base with God a little beforehand."

"Hmm," Paul pondered this unusual appearance of vulnerability in his stalwart friend. "You were brought up Catholic, right? Would you rather have a priest to talk with? I'm sure we could get the parish priest to stop by."

"No. I don't want to get all involved with the church. I just want a simple sacrament to pave the way to my heavenly rest."

"I'm happy to share communion with you, Betty, but I don't know the service of last rites, if that's what you're thinking about."

"That doesn't matter. I just think…I don't know. It would make Tess feel better, if she knew I'd tried."

"You don't do communion for other people. You do it for you."

"Fine, yes, I'm doing it for me. There, I said it. There are a few aspects of church life that I do miss, and communion is one of them. It would bring me great comfort," Betty used her most cajoling voice, and surprised herself by being quite sincere.

"Do you want to have Tess and the grandkids around you? We Protestants put high value on doing things in community."

"Oh, for heaven's sake, why does everything have to be such a big deal? Go get some wine and crackers and let's be done with it." Betty sounded momentarily like her old self.

Paul remained seated.

"I'm sorry," Betty apologized contritely. "I didn't mean to yell at you."

Paul still waited patiently.

"I've outlasted myself, Paul." She turned her head away so he wouldn't see the tears forming. "I guess with Christmas and New Year's coming up, it hit me. I'm overdue for the Grim Reaper and all

194

that." She turned back and met his kind eyes. "I'm scared. I don't want to go. I thought I did, that I didn't care. Last spring, in that place, I believed I wouldn't last another week, much less months and months. Then you all took me in, and things seemed brighter. But the dark is creeping in around the edges again."

"Now we're in familiar territory." Paul took her thin, cool hand in his warm one. "John 14:1. 'Let not your heart be troubled.' and John 8:12. 'I am the light of the world. Whoever follows me will never walk in darkness but will have the light of life.' It'll be okay, Betty. You'll see. You're safe with us."

"It's pretty scary, thinking about the end."

"We can talk about that. It doesn't help to keep it all inside."

"Don't tell Tess. She thinks I'm a tough old broad."

"I promise." Paul patted her arm reassuringly. "I'll get the others."

Paul brought crackers and a bottle of cabernet. He asked Ginny to bring some wine glasses and went to find his Pastoral Care visitation book.

Betty sat up on the edge of her bed, taking some deep breaths, considering all the care and love this foursome had offered her over the past six months despite her own occasionally ornery ways.

Arriving first to Betty's bedside and misunderstanding the reason for the impromptu gathering, Ginny filled the glasses half-full with the red wine while she waited. When the others came and Paul began the familiar words of the communion service, she sat beside Betty and put her arm around her. Luna, displaced from her usual spot at the foot of Betty's bed, curled up in her crate.

Betty received a cracker and then wine with her friends, the first swallow of liquid making a warm buzz down her throat, deep into her chest, and the next several sips reinforcing the cozy glow of love, friendship, and forgiveness.

"They'd get more people in your churches if they used this size glass instead of those teeny tiny things," Betty announced, savoring her final swallow.

"Our girl's back," Frank said with a smile.

Pulling the blankets up around her shoulders that night, and with Luna pleasantly heavy on her feet, Betty felt a new calm. She was ready to go, if that's what was in the cards. She tried to be quietly reflective, contemplative of her life, but new ideas kept intruding. She had *thought* she was ready to go. Or, maybe not. At any rate, the morning would decide. If she woke up, she'd have her answer.

Chapter Thirty-Eight

Ginny sat on the couch, the glow of the Christmas tree bathing the room in soft, colorful light. Each of them had settled into their favorite seat, letting their Christmas Eve dinner of salmon, rice, green bean casserole, and scalloped potatoes settle before attempting the apple and blueberry pies that were waiting. Lindsay and Mo, as well as Robert and Jill, were in the kitchen doing the dishes. The occasional clatter of dropped silverware indicated the younger grandchildren were assisting, too, while Lindsay's teens sat at the dining room table, plugged into their phones.

Ginny sighed in contented delight. Robert and Jill had allowed Francie and Mara to accompany them to the 4:00 Christmas Eve family service at church while they finished their own gift wrapping. The little girls had been enthralled with the 20-foot tree that nearly reached the ceiling of the sanctuary, the life-size wooden Nativity figures, the plethora of bright red poinsettias, and the singing of familiar carols. The outing was disaster free, other than a heart-stopping moment when little Francie's personal candle, lit for the singing of Silent Night in the darkened church, came perilously close to the long hair of the person standing in front of them. This, despite Frank's and her own unremitting surveillance of the lit fire sticks in the small hands.

Ginny checked her phone, then observed the mantel, decorated with boughs, battery-operated candles, family heirloom ceramic figures (safely out of reach), and sporting five stockings, neatly hung on tiny nails. Frank's train set-up ran around the tree's base, the little snow-covered houses invoking a miniature Christmas for imaginary families.

Ginny and Frank's stockings matched, purchased the first year they were married, 51 years ago. Paul and Joan each still had their distinctly different red wool stockings from childhood, now looking a bit moth eaten in the toes as they approached their 75th Christmases. Betty's was the largest and most elaborate stocking of them all, ordered online ten days ago once she had decided, in fact, she would live to see Christmas.

Ginny could hear Betty's voice and the excited sounds of her grandsons coming from the back of the house. After dinner, Tess, daughter Claire, and the younger boys had retreated to Betty's room so that Betty could read their favorite Christmas books to them, as was their holiday custom.

A new commotion ensued from the kitchen, and suddenly a parade appeared through the swinging door, led by little Francie and followed by Alex and his cousin Mara, who was carrying a three-layer cake slathered in vanilla icing and topped with red and green M&Ms.

"Surprise!" the children yelled in unison.

"Oh, my," Ginny said, taking in the blobs of white frosting dotting the girls' white-laced, green and red plaid Christmas dresses and Alex's good green shirt and red tie.

"M&Ms, my favorite!" Paul acknowledged approvingly.

"What a beautiful cake," Joan enthused.

"Let's head to the table," suggested Frank.

After passing the cake in front of each adult for their admiration, Mara pivoted quickly toward the dining room, caught her foot on the carpet and fell forward, planting herself squarely on top of the three-tier creation. After a few seconds of shocked silence, Mara pushed to her knees and erupted into a heartbroken wail, joined immediately by her little sister Francie. Alex tried gamely to help by picking up the cake platter and scraping some larger pieces of squashed cake and icing from his cousin's dress, as she remained frozen in place, sobbing.

Lindsay ran for paper towels while Robert and Jill comforted their broken-hearted children.

"At least she missed the train. Can we salvage the cake?" Frank asked hopefully. He hadn't been hungry for cake until the sugary apparition appeared before his eyes.

"There's an un-iced layer in the kitchen," Lindsay said, now desperately scraping white goo from the carpet. "At least this is vanilla icing. We'd never get chocolate stains out of the rug."

"Send in the dog," suggested Paul.

"No! The candy would be bad for her!" Joan was on her knees, too, gathering scattered, sticky M&Ms.

"Don't you just love Christmas?" Ginny asked no one in particular, glancing at her phone.

"Here," Lindsay handed her mother a gift after the mess was cleaned up. "You should probably open this before something else happens."

"What is it?" Ginny observed the square box with delight.

"You'll see."

Ginny tore off the wrapping and pulled out a large picture album. She opened it and discovered page after page of Christmas pictures, one for each year back to the first Christmas that she and Frank were married. Every tree, from the lopsided little ones up on a table out of reach of toddlers, to the giant one that had barely fit through the door. The trains, the stockings, the annual picture of kids in pajamas opening presents, it was all here. Christmas meals around the table, Paul and Joan and their younger son Joseph included once Mo and Lindsay had started to date. And the very last page had a picture of Betty in her hospital bed, holding the tiny decorated tree they had placed on Frank's desk, Paul and Joan standing beside her, all dressed in red shirts.

"How did you get these?" an amazed Ginny asked her daughter.

"Dad helped. When you were out of the house, I started going through the picture boxes. You are very well-organized, you know. It didn't take that long."

"I love it," Ginny got up from the couch and gave her daughter a warm hug. "Thank you so much. Now come on, I see Jill and the little decorators have patched together another cake. Let's eat."

The group moved to the table to have small pieces of the remaining cake layer and the dessert pies smothered in larger-than-usual scoops of ice cream. Ginny surreptitiously pulled her phone from her pocket and looked one more time.

"Why do you keep looking at your phone?" Frank asked from his seat beside her.

"I don't keep looking at my phone," Ginny replied quietly, sliding it back into her pocket.

"You've looked three times in the last half hour."

"No, I haven't."

"You have so, I've seen you."

"What are you watching me so closely for, all of sudden?"

"I'm not….Oh, never mind," Frank grumbled.

"I'll tell you later. Alex, dear, would you please go get Tess and tell her I need her for a minute?"

Tess came as bidden, just as the front doorbell sounded.

"Could you please get that?" Ginny asked her daughter's best friend.

Tess's face registered puzzlement, wondering why no one at the table could manage to get the door. Lindsay looked curiously at her mother, and then at Tess, and then, as the door swung open, to the bundled men standing on the doorstep.

"Surprise!" came shouts from multiple voices.

Tess stood frozen, then threw herself into her brothers' arms, while Ginny made her way to the door and pulled the boys and their families inside.

"Oh, my, gosh," Lindsay said to her father in wonder. "She did it, she actually did it. She got the boys to come."

"Who did what?" Paul asked from across the table.

"Mom did!" Lindsay said, going to her mother and wrapping her arms around her. "I can't believe you did it!" she whispered in her mother's ear before greeting the newcomers in the hallway. "Come on," Lindsay gathered the three young children, "let's go surprise your grandma!"

The group proceeded down the hall, and soon Betty's raspy exclamations could be heard all through the house.

Frank observed the packed den, a hubbub of noise and tears, Ginny tucked against the hallway wall and close to tears herself.

"Why is everyone crying?" Frank asked, having a déjà vu moment.

"Because, Frank. Just because."

It was after midnight by the time Ginny ushered Betty's sons and their families out the door to their hotel rooms, finished cleaning up the kitchen to her satisfaction, and had things ready for Christmas morning. She brought out the extra stockings for Betty's newly arrived grandchildren and hung them on the hearth. Four extra adults and three children for Christmas Day and dinner did not faze her; she was only hoping the little gifts she had bought the children would help make up for not having Christmas at home. She had been afraid to tell Betty ahead of time…if weather or some other unforeseen circumstance caused the cancellation of the cross-country trips, she feared the disappointment would be too much for her friend. On the other hand, Ginny had also worried the shock of the sudden appearance of her disappearing-act sons might trigger a heart attack. She had chosen to chance the latter, and hoped there were no Freudian agendas influencing her decision.

Frank was talking to her from the bathroom as she climbed wearily in bed, Christmas exhaustion overwhelming her.

"I can't believe you pulled that off, honey. I had no idea. Nice work."

"Hmm." Ginny's eyes were closing.

Frank crawled in beside her, kissing her forehead. "Who knew Santa was a travel agent?"

Ginny smiled, every muscle finally relaxing. "Wait till you see our credit card bill," she murmured. And with that, she was asleep.

Chapter Thirty-Nine

Six days after New Year's, on Thursday morning, Ginny and Frank stood in the doorway of Betty's room.

"Who's going to tell Tess?" Ginny asked her husband. "She's going to be here any minute. There's the doorbell now."

"I'll go," Frank said.

He opened the heavy front door just as Tess was about to ring again. Her happy, expectant smile fell as she saw the look on Frank's face.

"What is it?" Tess said.

"Tess," Frank said as kindly as he could, "your mom is gone."

"Oh, no," Tess burst into tears, hands cradling her face as she leaned into Frank's embrace.

"No, Tess, wait, I mean…oh, no, she's not dead. I shouldn't have said it that way. I'm sorry. I mean she's not here. She's not in bed."

"What?" Tess pulled back and looked at Frank uncertainly. "What do you mean?"

"Here," Ginny had arrived and held out a sealed envelope to their almost-daughter, while showing Frank a note addressed to them.

Tess took the note with shaking hands, still not comprehending. She had arrived expecting to pick her mother up to go out for a nice breakfast, then they were headed for an appointment with her attorney at ten o'clock. Tess had taken the morning off from work specifically for this meeting to go over her mother's will and end-of-life medical wishes, something her mother had been promising to do for months.

"Ours says," Ginny read, "that she is going with Scott to Snoqualmie Falls Inn for one last breakfast and a look at the waterfalls.

She'll take care of the attorney on her own, she'll be home after dinner, and she's taken her oxygen, so we're not to worry."

Tess's first reaction of grief was now turning into a growing rage. "Where's the dog?" she asked, barely able to contain herself.

Frank looked around. "I guess she took her. Her leash is usually here by the door."

"I can't believe it…she took the damn dog. Of course she did."

"Come in and sit," Ginny tried to pull Tess into the house.

"No. I'm done. I'm absolutely done. After all you did for her, getting the boys out here for Christmas, and now she pulls this kind of—" Tess handed her unopened note back to Ginny, turned around and went to the car. She slammed the door hard and Ginny and Frank watched helplessly as Tess bent over the steering wheel sobbing.

After lunch, Paul walked through the living room to get his car keys, dressed in his dark suit and dress shirt.

"Where are you going?" Joan asked him as the others looked up from the table. "You're looking rather pastoral."

"An appointment downtown. With Betty at her attorney's. She said I could tell you. Of course I didn't know when I agreed to go that Tess wouldn't be there."

"That woman makes me so angry, I could scream, sometimes," Ginny said. "It's as if she has no idea the hurt she causes with these thoughtless decisions."

"Oh, I bet she's put plenty of thought into it," Joan said. "Paul has seen all sorts of strange behavior around death and dying over the years. Denial and avoidance probably top the list, with the minister expected to pull the family back together again at the funeral."

"I'll see you all later," Paul excused himself quietly without commenting.

"See if you can at least bring home the dog," Ginny called to his back as he went through the front door. "It's too cold for Luna to sit in the car all day."

Late afternoon, Paul arrived home, a tired Betty on his arm and an enthusiastic Luna delighted to be off her leash. Joan wordlessly joined her husband and helped get Betty into bed. The day out seemed to have completely exhausted her, and wracking coughs came with more frequency.

"What were you thinking?" Joan asked her kindly as she pulled off wet clothes. "You shouldn't be out tromping around in this weather all day. You're damp all the way through. And your shoes are soaked."

"I know."

"Tess was disappointed."

"I know." Tears filled Betty's eyes as she sank onto the edge of the bed. "I couldn't face taking her to the attorney. It makes it so personal when she's right there." Betty paused for another coughing attack. "But Paul was wonderful. We got it all squared away."

"How about some tea or soup? We need to get you warmed up." Joan pulled a warm nightgown over Betty's head.

"Maybe later. I'll rest awhile. I guess I might have overdone it. But the falls were magnificent. I've never seen them with so much water flowing."

"All right," Joan tucked Betty in and pulled up the quilt, offering her a sip of water. "I'll check you in a while. Do you want the light off?"

"Yes, thank you. Is Ginny very angry?"

"Yes, I'd say so."

Betty closed her eyes. "Well, I wish you all could have seen the falls. They were magnificent."

Joan pulled the door shut.

"Is there a reason you're slamming the pots and pans around out here?" Frank asked his wife when he entered the kitchen. "There's nothing you can do about it, you know. She is the way she is, and it's how she's always been."

"I just can't watch Tess get hurt time after time. She's tried so hard."

Frank interrupted his wife's rough handling of the plates as she emptied the dishwasher to pull her into an embrace. "You know how they say an apple tree puts out a lot of fruit the year before it expires? Betty's putting out fruit, that's all. Everything she's got."

Ginny felt the anger she'd carried around all day begin to melt. "I think as far as Tess is concerned," she rested her head on Frank's shoulder, trying to hold back the tears that were welling up, "they're all crab apples. Not even good enough for one decent pie."

"I suppose so." Frank kissed his wife's head and then helped her start the meal.

Joan seemed to be making more trips to Betty's room than usual over dinner. Finally, she summoned Frank. "Betty wants to speak to you a minute," she said as Frank finished his dessert of leftover holiday cookies. "And here, take her this tea, would you please?"

Frank entered the darkened room and placed the mug of tea on the bedside stand. He pulled up the chair and regarded the seemingly ever-shrinking figure on the bed, the oxygen humming away as she took ragged breaths.

"I'm done in," Betty finally spoke, regarding her old friend.

"I can tell."

"What should I do? I don't want to stay like this. But I'm not seeing the exit door, either."

"Trying to catch pneumonia was an interesting choice. Was that your plan?"

"I don't know. I needed to get out. You know how I am, I like to be out."

Frank thought back to the first night when Betty had snuck out onto the patio. "We just had all that excitement of Christmas and New Year's. I thought that might hold you for a while."

"It was wonderful to have everyone here. Surely Ginny realizes how appreciative I am. I know she orchestrated the whole thing. The boys would never have brought their families without some prodding."

They sat silently for a while. Frank's attention was caught by the sound of a rose stem hitting against the house in the increasing wind and rain. The dark days were upon them now, the excitement of the holidays over, the short days of January promising only gloomy skies and rain until the first bulbs began pushing up in February.

"I think," Frank said deliberately, "I think it's time to call hospice. It's time to get some help for you, for all of us."

Betty was silent, and finally a tear slipped down her cheek. "I guess so. Maybe."

"They know how to help. To make you comfortable. Maybe how to talk with Tess. They know how to take the fear out of it, I think."

Betty took some more breaths, her eyes turning to the rain hitting the window pane in the dark.

"You think it would be good for Tess?"

"I do."

"All right. We'll call."

Frank breathed a long sigh.

"But not quite yet. We'll call Monday, okay? Give me the weekend to get used to the idea."

Frank took her hand and patted the tender skin gently. "Okay. We'll call on Monday. You promise?"

"I promise."

Chapter Forty

"So they called hospice?" Lindsay sat in her car Monday evening to get the news from Tess before entering the winter battle zone that her home became each January.

"This morning. It's going well, so far, I guess. Mom didn't panic at the first person through the door, so that's better than the last time."

"Did they say anything?"

"Your mom said they were a little surprised Mom was still living. I mean, I'm sure they didn't say that out loud, obviously. But that was your mom's sense of things." Tess was already in her kitchen, starting dinner, the phone on speaker on the counter top. Her anger at her mother had faded over the weekend. As always, she tried to understand how the very qualities she actually admired in her mom could make her mother so absolutely impossible to deal with at times.

"So, things are good between you, then?"

"I guess. I'll go over after dinner and check in. You know, Lindsay, I can't ever repay your parents for opening their home to my mom. We thought it would be for a couple weeks, and it's been over six months. That's so above and beyond...I can't even describe it."

Lindsay considered her own reluctant feelings about the decisions her parents had made over the past year: first inviting Mo's parents to move in, then accepting Betty into the fold. She grudgingly admitted it had worked out all right. And, in fact, it had actually been quite convenient to have all her kids' grandparents under one roof. And her best friend's mother, too.

Chapter Forty-One

Later that week, Ginny was sitting at her sewing machine mid-morning in the kitchen alcove when she heard a thump and then a sharp call from Betty and Luna barking. She rushed to the den and found Betty on the floor.

"Frank! Come help!" she called to the living room where she hoped her husband was probably reading the newspaper. "What on earth happened?" she directed to Betty, as she pulled back the heap of covers that had also fallen to inspect her friend for anything broken.

"I'm fine! I'm fine, just too weak to get up. Give me a hand, would you please?"

"Here I am," Frank arrived at the doorway. "What happened?"

"She fell out of bed," Ginny said.

"No, not exactly," a cranky Betty corrected Ginny. "I dropped the remote, and I wanted to get it without bothering anyone. But my legs gave out under me and I couldn't get back up. That's all. I'm fine. Just haul me back into bed."

Frank gently grabbed beneath her arms and lifted up.

Thankful they were not calling 911, Ginny slid the thin legs under the blankets, mumbling impatiently, "Honestly, Betty. Can't you ever stay in one place?"

"No. I really can't."

The quiet statement of extreme truth caught Ginny off guard. Looking into the tired face of her friend the annoyance she felt turned to compassion.

"Now if you don't mind looking for the remote...." Betty prompted.

Ginny dropped to her knees and found it under the bed. Plopping it into Betty's hands, she suggested dryly, "Next time, call us, okay?"

"I don't like having to call you for every little thing. It's ridiculous that my life has come to this state of affairs."

"Well," the practical Ginny observed the jumble of items on the bedside stand. "What would make things easier?"

"Nothing. But between the phone, the remote, my glasses, the water, and my book, something's always out of reach."

"Hmm." Ginny studied the situation thoughtfully. "I have an idea."

After an hour at her sewing machine, Ginny returned with a small quilt with pockets, each one perfectly sized to hold either the phone, the remote, Betty's glasses, her book, or pens and pencils.

"Look," Ginny said, placing the rectangular cloth across Betty's lap. "Now everything has a place and you can reach it without stretching to your bedside stand. And that clears up the bedside for your water glass."

Betty ran her hands over the new quilt appreciatively. "I love the colors and paisley pattern! It's perfect. And," she tucked her phone neatly into a pocket, "if I hadn't fallen out of bed, you'd never have thought of it!"

That afternoon, the hospice nurse remarked on the usefulness of Ginny's quilt, and mentioned how helpful such a coverlet would be to the other patients she visited. She even offered to buy some if Ginny would sew a few more. Ginny, whose sewing closet made her a top contender in the "She Who Dies With the Most Fabric Wins" contest, happily offered to donate some quilts. She had already decided that the pockets needed a small strip of Velcro to secure the contents a little better, considering the possible movement of the quilt on the bed.

Later, when Joan, who had been out on a Big Grandma assignment, examined the new quilt, she fingered the pockets thoughtfully.

"Do you think you could make some aprons with extra pockets like this? Fairly sturdy but ones that could be thrown in the wash easily? Think how helpful that would be for Big Grandmas...you'd have a place to keep your cell phone handy, maybe the house phone, the emergency numbers, first aid gloves, everything you need. What do you think?"

"Sure," Ginny said. "I'll play around with one tomorrow and you can see what you think."

"I've given you a new career," Betty said to Ginny.

"I didn't need a new career," Ginny replied, gathering up the dishes from the day in Betty's room, including Frank's coffee cup from the desk. But she was already planning how to make the most functional apron ever designed.

Chapter Forty-Two

Ginny had Alex along with her as she drove to the fabric store the next day after school. He was going to look at the wood crafts while she purchased Velcro and some elastic for her quilt and apron projects. And she hoped to find some kind of little hand bells to tie onto a corner of the quilts, as an easy way to call for help when needed.

It had been a windy day, with the house lights blinking threateningly several times during the morning. When she turned onto the main east-west thoroughfare, traffic was at a standstill. Looking ahead, she could see the traffic lights were out, so every intersection required a four-way stop. Creeping ahead slowly, she turned north at the next intersection, quickly revising her route to take advantage of side streets with no traffic lights and plotting a path that would bring her to the fabric store from another direction, avoiding the gridlock.

Alex's head had been in his book in the back seat, and when he looked up he didn't recognize the neighborhood. "Where are we, Noni?" he asked in a worried voice.

His apprehension and anxious look triggered a flashback to the day in the department store when Ginny had forgotten her grandson outside the shoe department. How much had happened since that awful moment when she realized she was without Alex. *What if that teenager hadn't been taking his grandmother to the doctor and hit Frank's car? What if we'd gone ahead and sold the house and moved? Where would Joan and Paul be now? And Betty?* An involuntary shudder brought her back to the moment.

"Don't worry, sweetheart," she reassured Alex. "I know where we are. Now tell me all about the wood kits you're hoping to find." She glanced again in the rear view mirror and watched his concerned look change to excitement as he described the build-your-own bird houses he had seen on the advertising flyer in the Sunday newspaper.

His enthusiasm warmed Ginny's heart, as always. He has Lindsay's eyes, she thought for the thousandth time. And his smile was just like Frank's.

Epilogue

Betty did eventually succumb to her ailments, but it was another four months, during three of which she continued to enjoy good quality of life, eating well, walking the dog, eschewing alcohol (most of the time) and cigarettes (all of the time), and enjoying the companionship and care of Ginny, Frank, Joan, and Paul. She made her peace with hospice care and gave herself over to their ministrations and support.

In appreciation of the loving care of her friends, Betty left a sizable donation to Big Grandmas and Grandpas as well as the local hospice organization. After her passing, Ginny, Frank, Joan, and Paul continued their quest to see all the Big Trees. The dog Luna remained at Ginny and Frank's house most of the time, unless they were traveling, when Tess took her.

Lindsay and Tess talked every day.

Acknowledgments

To my husband Richard, for manuscript help and loving support. To our adult children, Katie and Matt, Roxanne and Matt, Brian, and to Tori, for encouragement, manuscript readings, and technical help. To our joy-filled grandchildren.

To our parents, Peg, Ed, Jack, and Lois, whose qualities of courage, grace, common sense, and generosity infused my characters. They could have lived together happily.

To our friends and extended family; to the members of Faith Lutheran Church, Seattle, Washington; and to the members of the Church of the Good Shepherd, Olympia, Washington, all of whom cared for and supported our family during a medical crisis.

To the Faith Lutheran Church Women's Book Group, who for over twenty-five years have debated what makes a good read.

To Karla Petersen, tireless advocate for Big Brothers and Sisters, foster care, and adoption.

To Sheryl Schmeling and Nancy Estill who have kept me aware of the complicated issues surrounding homelessness.

For first draft manuscript reading: Kathy Brandstetter.

For help with manuscript details: Pastor Nancy Winder, Karen Millward, Pat Wilson.

For encouragement in staying the course in pursuing careers in the arts: Betsy Best.

For inspiration by example: Ken Shiovitz, biologist, philosopher, and poet.

To Cliff Mass, University of Washington meteorologist, for his excellent weather blog.

As always, all errors are my own.

Made in the USA
San Bernardino, CA
10 April 2019